Cider Days

An Ursula Nordstrom Book

Some Other Books by Mary Stolz

Cider Days

by Mary Stolz

Harper & Row, Publishers

New York, Hagerstown, San Francisco, London

Cider Days
Copyright © 1978 by Mary Stolz
Printed in the United States of America. For information address
Harper & Row, Publishers, Inc., 10 East 53rd Street, New York, N.Y.
10022. Published simultaneously in Canada by Fitzhenry & Whiteside
Limited, Toronto.

FIRST EDITION

Library of Congress Cataloging in Publication Data
Stolz, Mary Slattery, date
    Cider days.

    "An Ursula Nordstrom book."
    SUMMARY: A young girl's persistent overtures to a
new neighbor result in friendship.
    [1. Friendship—Fiction.   2. Family life—Fiction.
3. Vermont—Fiction]   I. Title.
PZ7.S875854Ci   [Fic]   77-25652
ISBN 0-06-025837-3
ISBN 0-06-025838-1 lib. bdg.

To Marcia and Lynne
at last, and far from least.

Cider Days

Chapter one

One of the best things to have is a best friend.

Unless.

Polly Lewis had had such a friend. Kate Willard.

"Do you realize," Kate had said one day last spring, "that we've been friends for eighteen years?"

Polly understood what she meant. She and Kate always understood each other. Just about. They were each nine years old and that came to eighteen years of sharing. Dolls and doll tea parties long ago. A tree house. A tarpaulin playhouse they'd built in Polly's barn. The platform of the tree house was still wedged in the oak tree where Polly's father had built it for them, but the tarp house no longer existed. They'd swum together, and ice-skated, and skied. They'd shared questions and secrets. They'd even shared the first day of kindergarten.

Polly remembered *that* day. She'd cried so hard that they'd called her mother at the doctor's office where Mrs. Lewis worked, and her mother had driven to the school to take her home. Only by that time Kate had patted and coaxed her into staying, and from that day Polly had liked school. Sometimes she wondered how things would've turned out if Kate hadn't been there.

The first day of school, even kindergarten, maybe especially kindergarten, was important. If it went all wrong, if you were scared and upset by so many kids and a stranger called a teacher and a big strange room, and there wasn't anybody like Kate there to make you stop crying and *notice* things—the aquarium with its flashing fish and frondy weeds, the coloring books, the blocks with numbers and letters on them—why then you might just get taken home crying on the first day. And after that maybe school would always be something that made you want to cry. She knew kids who still got sick to their stomachs every year on the first day of school. But she had had Kate Willard.

In their eighteen years together, nine apiece, they'd exchanged probably trillions of words, both being champion talkers. Polly had a bed in Kate's room called "Polly's," and Kate had one in Polly's room called "Kate's." They'd shared music lessons, and all sorts of plans and ideas and even, sometimes, fears. They'd sat together in the school yard at lunchtime and chosen each other to be on teams when the chance arose. They'd shared Polly's little horse, Blondel. (At any rate, enough so that Kate would ride double on him when they wanted to go on a picnic away from the house. Kate never rode him alone.)

There were—there were too many shared things to count or remember. And now they were just to miss.

Having a best friend is great. Unless. Or until.

Polly, sitting on the fence across from her house, watching Blondel canter around the meadow teasing Mr. Ingalls' cattle, sighed. It was great to have a best friend unless or until the best friend moved to California, leaving you behind in a village where you knew every single person and didn't have anybody to call up.

Here it was, the week before the first day of fifth grade, and she didn't know anyone to call and ask, "What're you going to wear on Monday?"

She and Kate had always done that. Polly could even remember what they'd worn the year before, on the first day of fourth. Kate had had a new blue jersey jumper with a blue-and-white-checked shirt. Polly had worn an old vanilla-colored sweater and a new camel-colored skirt. And early on that early September morning, Polly had biked down the hill as usual, across the covered bridge, up the hill on the other side to Kate's house. And then they'd gone on to school, riding side by side when traffic permitted, or one behind the other, but always talking, talking, both of them at once, neither having any trouble following what the other was saying, although grown-ups listening to them claimed not to understand how they did it.

"How can you hear what she's saying when you're gabbing every second yourself?" Mrs. Lewis would ask Polly. "And vice versa, of course." Polly had said she didn't know. They just did.

This year Polly hadn't decided what to wear on the first day of school, and she hadn't bothered to ask her mother for anything new. She sat scowling on the fence because once again the mail had come and once again there had been nothing for her.

When Kate and her family and Kate's cat, Puffpuff, had left for California, driving all the way, Polly had written some letters to greet Kate upon her arrival. So she wouldn't feel so lonesome out there without any friends. So she'd know her friend at home was remembering her. She'd given Kate plenty of time to answer, figuring how long the drive took, and then the settling in and all. But it was weeks now, and Kate had never even sent a postcard.

"Well," said Polly out loud. "Oh, well."

She fingered the whistle she carried in her sweater pocket for calling Blondel to her side, then changed her mind. She thought of calling up Consuela, but changed her mind. Consuela Christina Machado. Polly could call her and ask what she was going to wear to school. But she wouldn't. Consuela, whose mother wore the most *dashing* outfits, was not the least bit interested, herself, in clothes. It was difficult to figure out what Consuela was interested in. It was funny that someone you let ride your horse two or three times a week still wasn't somebody you could call up and ask, "What are you going to wear next Monday?"

Consuela and her famous mother, the painter Moya O'Shea, had a telephone, and sometimes answered it. Sometimes they didn't. Polly had been at their house when it rang and neither of them made a move toward it and just let it ring itself out. She could not understand that. There was so much about Consuela and her mother that was hard to understand that it was easier to think about what you could understand. *Sort* of understand.

She knew, the whole town knew, that Moya O'Shea was divorced from Consuela's father, who was a Mexican doctor. She knew that Consuela preferred her father's name to her mother's. And maybe her father to her mother, although Consuela had never said that. She didn't say that, and she didn't say much of anything else. She was the most silent girl Polly had ever known.

6

Polly, who talked a lot, sometimes felt *chattery* when she was with Consuela. It made her uneasy, but never stopped her from talking.

Still, there it was, and it all came out to the same thing: nobody to telephone about Monday's clothes. There was Sandra Rutledge. Or Faith Jennings. There was even Betty Sackett, if a person was positively desperate. Sandra and Faith were nice and probably wouldn't mind at all if she telephoned them. But she wasn't going to. Betty was boy-crazy and had talked Kate into deciding to be boy-crazy, too, and that had caused the only real quarrel she and Kate had ever had, and just before she was moving away, too.

"Oh, darn," said Polly.

She remembered her mother and Gram warning her and Kate once in a while that if they didn't branch out a little, make other friends besides each other, they might be sorry sometime. She and Kate had listened and gone on being best friends not needing anybody else.

Okay, so now she was sorry. But how was she to know that Kate would move to California and then not even bother to write? How was she to know that Gram and her mother would be right when they told her it'd be hard to form new friendships with people you hadn't seemed to give much of a darn for all these years?

Consuela and her mother had come to town, just after Kate left, to live in a marvelous house Ms. O'Shea had had built on a hillside a couple of miles away. Polly had had a spurt of hope then. She'd befriended Consuela—Connie, as most people called her, even though she didn't like it. Polly had figured that Consuela would be even lonelier than she was herself at that time. After all, it would only take a little gumption, a little pride swallowing, for her to make motions toward people. She *knew* everybody here. But Consuela had come up from Mexico. From a Texas border town, really, where she'd been living with her parents. Her father had a clinic there for Mexican workers. But Consuela had grown up in Guadalajara. Vermont was a foreign land to her and she didn't know anybody at all. So Polly had made the first move. Inviting Consuela to ride double on Blondel down to the village fair one evening in early August. She'd been so pleased to have somebody liking Blondel— Kate never really had, for all she'd *tried*—that she'd blurted an offer to let Consuela ride him sometimes if she wanted to.

Blurting. That was one of her main troubles. Talk first, think later. Dope. Double dope. Blurting was one of the reasons she was always fighting with her kid brother, Rusty. Rusty was an unearthly pest, as anybody but her family could see, but if she'd only learn to keep her mouth shut when he said his asinine stupid things, if she'd learn to walk away when he got into one of his tantrums, then she'd be—she'd be *superior* to him. It was dreadful and mortifying for somebody her age to get into scraps with a horrid little boy of seven. Sometimes they actually tangled and once Gram had dumped a pail of cold water on them, the way you would on a couple of scrapping cats. Just awful, awful, awful . . .

She didn't *mind* letting Consuela ride Blondel. Consuela was a good rider. Very good. And she took proper care of Blondel, rubbing him down, walking him, after a ride. She brought grain for him once a week. Not that she'd been asked to. And she loved him. Polly couldn't resist anyone who loved Blondel. Nevertheless, it hadn't worked out to a friendship. Consuela was too darned quiet. Shy, Gram said. Sadly shy, and you should feel sorry for her, not for yourself, Polly. You have no idea what a handicap it is to be as shy as Consuela is.

Gram was probably right. She usually was. But it leaves me, thought Polly, with no friends and no mail and no new clothes for school, and I can feel sorry for myself if I want to.

She fingered the whistle again. She wondered whether to go across the road to the barn and get Blondel's bridle and go for a short ride, or even his saddle and take a long one.

How could anybody feel sorry for herself who had Blondel, and who had a family she adored (if you left out Rusty which she'd have liked to do but couldn't) and a dear old dog and a dear young cat and who lived in Vermont—

"Polly! Polly, come over, will you?"

Her mother was on the kitchen porch, calling, and Polly leaped lightly from the fence, remembering that it was Wednesday, therefore her mother's day off, so maybe they were going to do something that was fun.

Chapter two

The house George and Anna Lewis had been lucky enough to find twelve years before, when they'd moved to Vermont where Mr. Lewis was to teach in a college ten miles away, was dated 1805. It was built of brick, of a beautiful rosy shade that bricks didn't come in anymore. Attached to the house was a shed that Gram said had probably been used as a summer kitchen in the olden days. The Lewises used it to store wood for the winter. Attached to the shed was a vast barn that had once housed farm implements, and cattle in the wintertime when snow, with drifts, would go as high as eight or nine feet. Now Anna Lewis kept her Volkswagen in it. There were also garden tools, a sled, skates, skis, old pieces of furniture, boxes, trunks, an ancient hay baler, coils of rope, maple syrup cans, more wood in case the supply in the shed ran out. The shed and the barn were made of clapboard and painted red.

The house had a front door with an old brass knocker shaped like a fox's head and a beautiful fanlight over the top. That door was just about never used. The kitchen was the center of the house and everybody, even company, used the kitchen door.

The kitchen was a big room, with a window looking over the back meadow and a padded window seat beneath. There was a large wooden table in the center and Polly sometimes thought you could call that table the house's heart. They ate around it. They played cards or did jigsaw puzzles at one end. Gram, who did all the cooking, did most of her preparing on it. Polly did her homework on it. Rusty, too. When he bothered to do any. There was a big cast-iron wood stove in one corner. All the rooms in the house had wood stoves and Mr. Lewis, who was not only a conservationist but also frugal, turned on the central heating only when winter had bitterly settled in, around Christmastime. Sometimes he relented for visitors unaccustomed to Vermont weather. But the Lewises were used to living with wood stoves. At this time of year, the first week in September, they hadn't been used at all. Polly loved it when on that first morning Gram would say, "Well, George, I think this morning calls for a fire," and, without waiting, would crumple up some newspaper, toss in a few pieces of kindling, then carefully lay on a large piece of maple, or apple, or oak, and in moments a woodsy warmth would be filling the kitchen.

But that would not be for a while yet. Now the screen door wasn't even down. Polly came into the kitchen and found her grandmother at one end of the table cutting up early windfalls for applesauce and her mother at the other end making a marketing list.

She took a piece of apple. Crisp, sharp, sweet. "Pretty soon we can make cider, Gram."

"Another two or three weeks, we certainly can."

"I like seasons. Consuela says it's always hot in Mexico.

11

That'd be awful."

"Probably not if you grew up in such a climate," said Gram, who did not like hot weather but was willing to be fair about it provided she could live in Vermont. Vermont could get pretty hot in the summer, but not for long.

"Polly—" said Mrs. Lewis, as Polly was saying, "Mom—"

They stopped, waited, then as her mother waited longer and Polly could rarely hold her silence, she said, "Mom, what I want to know—and Gram, too—is why you, I mean we, haven't ever invited Ms. O'Shea and Consuela to supper. I mean, I don't think it's polite. Anybody else new in town you'd have asked. Especially since *I've* had tea there with them. Twice."

"Well, Polly, we figure she must be pretty busy. Such an important person. I understand she's been asked to several houses, people who want to give parties for her, and she always says no. Your father says half the faculty has made overtures and been rebuffed. No point asking to be rebuffed."

"I don't think she'd rebuff us. She likes us. She told me she did."

"I'm sure she likes you, dearie," said Gram. "But she doesn't even know the rest of us. I've seen her whizzing through town on that motorcycle of hers, but she's never slowed down actually to speak to me. She does smile and wave," the elder Mrs. Lewis admitted. "As if she recognized me. How she dares take a hand off that thing I don't know."

"Of course she *recognizes* you," Polly said irritably.

"How?"

"Oh, Gram. She met you at the Fair in August."

"No. Your father and mother have met and talked with her, but I haven't."

"Well, then she's seen you on the porch or something. She always asks about you. She thinks you look dramatic."

Her grandmother smiled. She was a very tall thin woman who dyed her hair black and wore makeup. Polly could tell she liked being called dramatic.

"I *think* we should invite them for supper."

"Well," said Anna Lewis, "no point in rushing things. After she settles in, we'll see. How are you and Connie getting along?"

"She wants to be called Consuela. I told you. And I don't know how we're getting along. I know she likes Blondel but I haven't found out yet if she likes me."

"That poor child," said Mrs. Lewis. "She puts me in mind of a long-legged, long-necked, solemn and altogether gorgeous bird."

"Solemn? You mean because she doesn't talk?"

"I mean because she's so unhappy. Anyone can see that if she could she'd wing her way to Mexico without looking back."

"They were living in Texas. Where her father has the clinic for the Mexican workers."

"She misses her father, I'm sure. But I get the feeling that what she's really sick for is Mexico. Just suppose, Polly, that you were suddenly sent to Guadalajara—that's where she's from, isn't it?—suppose you were sent there and didn't know if you'd ever get back to Vermont. How would you feel?"

Polly frowned. She looked out the window across to

their meadow, where Mr. Ingalls grazed his cattle and Blondel was, at that moment, having a happy solo canter. She looked around this kitchen, at her grandmother's deft hands quartering apples, at her mother's sweet face with blond hair tied back. She stroked Chino, who was purring beside her on the window seat, and studied Okie, the old collie, sprawled across the floor in everybody's way as usual. Leave it, all this? Go to Mexico and maybe never come back?

"I'd hate it. But if you were with me, Mom—"

"Just me? No rest of the family? No Vermont hills and seasons? Besides, you and I get along pretty well, most of the time. You say Consuela and her mother don't even have that going for them."

Polly supposed she shouldn't have told. It was true. Consuela and her mother didn't get along together. The two times Polly had been at their house, it seemed to her that Ms. O'Shea *tried*, but the more she tried the stiffer Consuela became. Just the same, she shouldn't have told. Was there some way a person could get over being such an awful blabbermouth? Once she'd made a pact with herself not to tell anything about anybody to anyone for at least a week, and by the end of the morning had been telling Kate about her and Rusty fighting all over the kitchen floor and getting cold water dumped on them. You'd think something so humiliating would be easy enough to keep quiet about, but oh, no—

"I just hope," she muttered, "that nobody ever tells me an important secret, that's what I hope," and was surprised when her mother leaned over and hugged her.

"Look," said Mrs. Lewis, "my idea is that today being Wednesday, and the last week that the Thespian Society is giving its play for young people, we could drive into town and have lunch at the Cheese Garden and then drop Rusty off and you and I could shop and find you something nice to wear for the first day of school. What do you say?"

"That's super!" Polly turned to her grandmother. "Gram, you come with us."

"No, thank you, love."

"But why *not?*"

"Because I choose not to. Lunching at the Cheese Garden is not my idea of earthly bliss. Besides, I want to make a couple of pies from these apples."

"But you never go anyplace."

"I go lots of places. I have my bridge night, don't I? I go to the concerts at the college, don't I? And last month, as I recall, we ate out at some church supper or other two or three times a week. That's enough going out for me for some time to come."

Polly knew that her grandmother meant what she said.

"But it—looks to other people like we just use you as a cook," she mumbled.

"Who said that?" Anna Lewis asked sharply.

Polly wriggled. "Oh well—it was Kate. Not Kate, really. She said her mother said it."

"That silly Mrs. Willard," said Gram. "The woman has no insight at all. I do precisely what I choose to do in this household, and if what I choose to do is cook, as Mrs. Willard chooses to do exquisite needlework, then it's my affair. Furthermore, I doubt if many people are gossiping about my role in life. If they were I certainly would not alter the way I do things simply in order to stop them. Fact is, Polly, I don't give a hoot what people say, and neither should you."

"I'll give a hoot, if you'll tell me what to hoot about," said Rusty, coming in and banging the door behind him. "Fact is, Polly, I'll hoot even if *nobody* tells me what to hoot about. Hoot, hoot, hoot, hoooot, HOOT—"

"Mom! Make him stop!" said Polly, covering her ears.

Rusty continued to hoot, head thrown back, hands dangling and wriggling at his sides. He looked and sounded like a fool and Polly could not and never had been able to figure out why people thought he was good-looking. That stupid carroty hair, that face that was always being screwed up into gruesome expressions, that—that—

"Hoot, hooooot, hoothoothoot—"

"Mom!"

The two Mrs. Lewises were watching the hooter with interest. Anna Lewis flapped a silencing hand at Polly. They were going to wait and see how long he could keep it up. Once Rusty had decided it'd be fun to have a husky voice and had tried to shout himself into one. After about ten minutes of shouting, Mr. Lewis had sent him out of the house to the back meadow to continue his experiment there. He'd scared the cattle and got Okie howling so wildly that neighbors had begun to call up in alarm. And still nobody had tried to stop him. Finally, he'd run down, leaving his voice the same as before. Polly had had embarrassing explanations to make to Kate, who'd heard the racket all the way over at her house and called up to find out what was doing.

Kate had thought it was funny. "He gets the nuttiest ideas, doesn't he?" she'd said, sounding impressed.

And here they were now, Gram and her mother, letting him hoot like a banshee, making no effort to stop

16

him. Suddenly, before anyone knew what she planned, Polly went to the sink, filled a two-cup measure with water, turned and dashed it in her brother's face. "There!" she said. "That's what we—"

Rusty flung himself at her, the measuring cup flew from her hand and broke against the stove, Gram and Mrs. Lewis each seized one of them and held them, struggling, apart.

"Lemme at her!" Rusty shouted. "I'll kill her!"

"Stop it, Rusty," Anna Lewis said, holding him with some difficulty. For his age, Rusty was strong, and rage was lending him extra power. But his mother hung on while Gram, holding Polly's shoulders, said, "What in the world gets into you two? Polly, what right had you to—"

"But Gram—that's what you did to us when we were fighting. You said it was the only way to bring two wild animals to their senses. He's a wild ani—"

"Polly! There are some things that only adults can do, *however* reluctantly. I did not enjoy throwing water on the two of you that day, but you were past all reasoning and might have hurt each other—"

"I did," said Polly with satisfaction. "I blacked his eye."

"I'll black yours," Rusty growled. "You just wait. I'll black your both eyes."

"He was *hooting* past all reason," Polly complained. "He sounded like a crazy person."

"He was just being silly. His father used to behave like that."

This was an odious suggestion that Polly did not for a moment accept. Gram was saying it to make her feel ashamed of throwing water in Rusty's face. Well, she wasn't ashamed. And her father had never in his life, even when he was a little boy, acted like this—this *worm*.

"We're waiting for you to apologize, Polly," said her mother, but Rusty said calmly, "Lemme go, Mom. She's a nitwitty girl. I don't pay attention to nitwitty girls. She wouldn't mean any apology anyway."

This was of course true, but the way Rusty always got over his rages so easily made Polly feel inferior, insecure and furious.

Anna Lewis looked at her dripping son, her wild-eyed daughter. "Give me strength," she said to the ceiling. "Rusty, go change into dry clothes and comb your hair. That is, if you'd like to have lunch with Polly and me at the Cheese Garden. Then you can see *Pinocchio*. It's the last week of the Thespian Society's—"

"Hey, hey," said Rusty. "That's neat. What'll I wear?"

"Something clean, for a preference."

"Sure, sure." Rusty dashed up the back stairs in high good humor and Polly looked after him, her teeth set.

Gram took the dustpan and broom from the closet, but Polly snatched them from her and swept up bits of broken glass from the floor.

"Sorry I broke it," she snarled and waited for one of them to ask if she was sorry about anything else. This time they didn't. They'd decided to be understanding. Sometimes Polly thought she wouldn't be able to *stand* how much understanding there was around this house.

"It's not *fair*," she yelled. "He always starts every-thing—"

"Oh, tut," said her grandmother.

"Well, he does too—"

18

"No," said her mother. "He doesn't. The fact is," she said thoughtfully, "I'm not sure either of you starts things. I think there's a term in biology called antipathetic symbiosis, which means that two organisms are mutually destructive—"

"That's not it, precisely," said Gram, who'd been a teacher long ago, in a college in Maine. "Antipathetic symbiosis is generally a parasitic situation, where one organism destroys the other but remains intact itself—"

How could anybody be expected to put up with this? Polly thought despairingly. "I'm not going with you. You go see *Pinocchio* with Rusty and have lunch with Rusty and—" She had to bat her eyelids quickly to keep from crying. She did not like to cry in front of people, any people. She started out of the room and ran right into her grandmother, who held her close and said, "There, there, dearie. It's trying. We know. But we are a family, and we do have to try to get along, don't we now?"

Polly sniffled, nodding her head against her tall grandmother's skinny front.

"So." Gram gave a releasing hug, smiled and said, "Why don't you go up and comb your hair and think about what you'd like to buy for school next week. I suggest something with a lot of red in it. Nothing like wearing red to increase self-confidence."

Taking a deep breath, Polly nodded again, smiled weakly at her grandmother and mother and went upstairs to get ready for the treat. Rusty had a way of spoiling things. But if she were smart—if she tried anyway to be smart—she wouldn't *let* him. He never let anything she did spoil his fun. Lunch at the Cheese Garden was a treat she adored and she was not going to let that worm

19

ruin everything—

The worm came out of his room, hair slicked back, wearing a clean cotton jersey and clean shorts. Underneath the clean things he had an unwashed smell and his neck was dirty.

"Hey, this's fun, huh, Poll?" he said cheerfully. "Why'n't you come and see *Pinocchio* too?"

With an effort of will, Polly smiled. How *did* he do it? How did he *do* it? He couldn't just be putting it on. He really did recover his good spirits as easily as he lost them. "I've seen it twice, thanks. But we'll have fun at the Cheese Garden. Won't we?"

"Sure thing," said Rusty and slammed down the stairs, leaping the last five and landing with a tremendous thud.

Polly followed more slowly, kissed her grandmother good-bye, went out to the car where Rusty and her mother were waiting, he in the backseat as always.

They set out for the treat.

Chapter three

They sat in the "garden" part of the restaurant, outdoors in the back, considering themselves lucky to have got a table there on such a wonderful Indian summer day.

"Not that it's all that gardeny," Polly said, looking at the crowded-together tables jammed with students and teachers from the college where Polly's father taught English and where her mother was a nurse in the Medical Faculty Building.

Beneath them was gravel and there wasn't a flower to be seen and never were any, even in summer. But maples and oaks and sycamore trees stretched their branches overhead and now and again a mild gust of air released bright leaves that floated to the tables beneath. As she spoke, an oval lemon-colored leaf settled gently on top of her chocolate milk. She plucked it out, licked it and said reflectively, "Just the same, it's awfully nice."

"Who said it wasn't?" Rusty asked. His voice was not especially quarrelsome and Polly ignored him.

She looked at her mother, and thought that she could practically be taken for one of the college girls. So blond and pretty and—darling. Polly was proud of her.

"You look nice," she said.

"Thanks a heap," said her brother.

"I wasn't—" Polly caught her lip just before falling into his childish trap. Rusty grinned at her knowingly.

Suddenly there was a rustle at the other tables. Everyone was looking at the door that led to the "garden."

There stood Moya O'Shea. Ms. O'Shea, famous artist, mother of Consuela Christina Machado. She stood as if framed in one of her own paintings, tray in hand, gazing about to see if there was a place for her.

She wore a tangerine jump suit, very tight fitting, with white stripes down the side, a white scarf at her throat. Dangling in the crook of her elbow was a gleaming white motorcycle helmet. Goggles, white rimmed, were shoved up, holding back her dark, shining, carelessly curling hair.

"My word," said Anna Lewis. "It's like something out of *Star Trek*."

"I think she's gorgeous," Polly breathed.

So, apparently, did many of the young men present, since at least a dozen leaped to their feet, indicating that Ms. O'Shea could have their places, and—from their expressions—anything else she happened to want.

With a gracious, grateful, general smile for all, Ms. O'Shea made her way through the crowded garden restaurant tables to where the Lewises were sitting.

"Suppose I could squeeze in here?" she murmured confidently.

Polly had jumped up at her approach. "She can have my chair, okay, Mom?"

"But you haven't finished your—" Mrs. Lewis looked up. "Hello. How are you? I don't see—"

A boy with a frail bobbing beard sprang from his place at the next table and thrust his chair at Ms. O'Shea, who took a tighter grip on her tray even as she reduced him to near tears with her smile.

"Please," he begged, as Polly and her mother moved to make room at the table. "*Please* take my seat."

"So kind," said Ms. O'Shea, sitting down with her back to him. Not her fault, Polly thought. It's the way the chair is facing. But she couldn't help feeling sorry for the boy, who picked up his beer and sandwich and gave a last hopeless look at Moya O'Shea before wandering to a corner of the garden where, at last, somebody made room on a bench for him.

Polly saw him seated, then forgot him as thoroughly as Ms. O'Shea clearly had. She was unwrapping an enormous ham-and-cheese sandwich, opening a carton of milk. She also had a cherry tart on her tray.

"How in the world do you keep your figure?" Anna Lewis asked in a faintly irritable tone.

"Jogging." Ms. O'Shea licked mustard from the corner of her mouth. "Five miles a day."

Anna Lewis, who had a trim figure herself and had to watch it and hated exercise, looked at the remains of her cottage cheese and fruit salad, her black coffee no sugar, and said determinedly, "Well, Ms. O'Shea—are you and Consuela all settled in?"

"Yes, yes. Working again. Such a relief. I do wish you'd call me Moya. We haven't seen each other since—since the night of the Fair, isn't it? But Polly here has been to tea, and *she* calls me Moya. So dear about lending Connie her horse, too."

Mrs. Lewis looked at her daughter and Polly looked away. Actually she'd found it easy, after the first few tries, to call Ms. O'Shea *Moya*. But she hadn't bothered to tell them at home. Gram and her parents puzzled her. In some way, they didn't seem to care for Moya O'Shea. Exciting, famous, beautiful, friendly Moya. Besides, she knew a lot of kids who called adults by their first names. She even knew a couple—Betty Sackett and her brother—who called their parents by firsts. Not to be thought of around her own house.

"Where's Consuela?" she asked.

"Home. She wouldn't come with me because I took the bike. Connie can be persuaded to ride the Honda, but not easily. Not unless there is no other conceivable way to get where she wants to go—"

"Unaccountable," Anna Lewis said, almost to herself.

Moya O'Shea apparently didn't hear. She went on, "Today she said she'd pass. I just wanted to run into town to the Senior Art Exhibit. See what sort of things they're up to, the young ones."

"What did you think of their work?" Mrs. Lewis asked.

"Some of it's marvelous," Moya O'Shea said enthusiastically. She finished her sandwich, started on the cherry tart. She had a milk mustache that she didn't bother to lick off.

"Moya," said Rusty, as if he'd been calling her that all his life, "Moya, is your motorcycle in the parking lot?"

"Right there."

"Can I sit on it for a second, huh?"

"Sit on it? Wait till I finish this and I'll give you a ride on it."

"Oh, boy! Oh, man!" Rusty shrieked. "Oh, hollering catfish!" He was, literally, jumping up and down. He waved his arms. Joy pealed in every syllable, flashed in his eyes. Delight, astonishment, enfolded him. One little question and one little answer had tumbled him headlong into heaven. And then came his mother's voice.

"It's—it's *kind* of you to offer," said Anna Lewis forbiddingly. "But we're taking Rusty to see *Pinocchio* now. And we'll be late if we don't leave immediately. So nice to have seen you, Ms. O'Shea." She rose. "Children—"

"I don't want to see *Pinocchio*! Dumb stupid play. I want to ride on Moya's motorcycle!"

"Out of the question."

"But *Mom*—"

"You will not ride on a motorcycle, Rusty. Not today, not tomorrow, not ever as far as I'm concerned."

Wiped out, erased, dashed from the heights to the sunless bottom of the deepest pit, Rusty stared, not believing that the prize on which he'd almost put his fingertips could be snatched from him in this fashion. He looked at his mother and his face grew dark.

Polly felt her stomach muscles tighten. This was going to be awful. It was going to be terrible and unbearable. She was tempted to desert her mother, who was glaring at Ms. O'Shea, and run for the comparative safety of their car in the parking lot.

She glanced at her brother, hoping that just this once, just because they were out and not in the privacy of their house, *just this once* he wouldn't have a tantrum because things hadn't worked out his way. Please, Rusty, she prayed silently. Please, please, just this once—

Rusty swallowed hard. His face became a cementlike mask with slitted burning eyes. He opened his mouth. From it issued a howl so piercing that a girl three tables away knocked her Coke over.

"What's *that*?" she quavered, looking around, and then every eye in the garden was on Rusty.

Fists clenched above his head, he was shrieking at his mother, "I tell you, I am too gonna ride on the b-b-bike! I am too, and you're not gonna stop me, hear? You aren't, you aren't, you aren't. You horrible dopey dumb mother. You're the worst mother I ever had in my whole life."

Polly, amazed and furious, could tell her mother was trying not to smile. "That may be," she said evenly. "But if you don't care to see the play, you are coming with Polly and me." She looked at Moya O'Shea. "Thanks a *heap*."

"But what's this all about? I'm a careful—"

"I'm going with her, I tell you! I'm gonna ride on the m-m-motorcycle with her and you aren't gonna—"

"No," said Moya O'Shea. "You are not going to ride on it." She finished the last swallow of milk, patted her lips with a paper napkin. "I don't take crazy people riding with me. *You* are acting crazy."

Rusty teetered.

Polly, watching, could feel herself inside his head, where he was trying to decide on a course. Go ahead with the tantrum? She knew from experience how hard it was to stop, once started. But—if stopping would get him on the motorcycle? If stopping would cause Moya to say, Okay, you aren't crazy, come along? But then the voice of authority, the horrible mother voice would cut in again and deprive him of his chance at heaven—

Rusty went on screaming.

Now everybody was looking away from him. People were trying to talk and act normally, as if this crazy boy wasn't in their midst, jumping up and down, yelling words that probably everybody knew, but nobody in our house, Polly thought, her face dully glowing, ever *says*.

"Rusty, stop," she whispered. "That's—awful. Stop saying those things."

Rusty couldn't hear her. He couldn't stop. He didn't notice when Ms. O'Shea, picking up her white helmet, carried her tray to the dumbwaiter and walked off with a casual "So sorry" flung over her shoulder. He couldn't feel his mother's hard grip on his shoulder.

Polly, squeezing her arms together, considered again whether to desert and run.

"Rusty," said Mrs. Lewis, leaning over to speak in her son's ear, "I am giving you five seconds to stop this behavior. Five. I'm starting to count *now*. One—two—three—" She straightened. Rusty glanced upward, studying her face, his own still contorted. "—four—"

Drawing a deep rattly breath, Rusty shuddered into comparative silence. In that silence the three of them left the Cheese Garden. Polly knew she heard a burst of laughter following.

On the sidewalk outside, Mrs. Lewis looked at her two children dispiritedly, rallied, smiled and said, "Well, what about it? Shall we drop you off at the theater, Rusty?"

"No."

"I see. It's the last chance you'll have to see *Pinocchio*."

"Don't wanna see it."

"I see," Mrs. Lewis repeated. "All right, then. Do you want to come shopping with—"

"Mom, honestly, I don't feel like getting anything new for school. I—just don't feel like it." Polly was sorry the treat had been spoiled by her cockroach of a brother, but there it was—spoiled.

"What would you like to do?"

Rusty said nothing.

"Go home," said Polly. She wanted to get home as fast as possible and get Blondel's saddle out and go for a ride to nowhere, seeing no one.

On the way, Rusty, in the back, kicked his feet against the seat in front, which was Polly's.

"Cut it out, Rusty."

He curled his upper lip.

"If you're *trying* to look fierce, it doesn't work. Not with two teeth missing. You just look like a fool, you fool. . . ."

"Stop it, Polly," said Mrs. Lewis.

"*Me?*" Polly was outraged. "*Me* stop it? Who embarrassed us to darn death right out in front of the public gaze, I ask you? Why should I stop telling him what I think of— Rusty! Quit kicking the seat or I'll—"

"Yeah? You'll just what, huh? Just you'll *what*, Pilly-Polly?"

"I'll slam you, that's what."

"Oh boy. That's one big haw-haw. *You'll* slam *me*! In a pig's eye, you'll—"

"Cut it out! Stop it, both of you, do you hear me?"

Rusty gave a last hard kick at the back of Polly's seat. Polly folded her arms and looked ahead.

In a little while, Mrs. Lewis said, "Rusty, I realize that you would think it seventh heaven to ride on that death contraption—don't interrupt—but you happen to be a cherished member of this family—"

"Count me out," Polly muttered.

"—a *most* cherished member," Mrs. Lewis went on. "And I don't intend to let you risk your life on a motorcycle, and that's that. I'm just telling you not to come whining around trying to get permission, because you are never going to get it."

"How about when I'm grown up, huh?"

"Maybe when you're fifty, I'll reconsider. If you behave every single minute from now until then."

Rusty laughed. "Hey," he asked. "What would you have done if I'd gone on hollering back there, huh? I mean, if you'd got to *five*?"

"Never you mind. It was something pretty horrid, count on that. I think I'll save it for next time."

"How d'ya know there'll be a next time?"

"Same way I know winter will come."

"Maybe I'll fool you."

"I'll be the first to be delighted if you do."

"And then would you let—"

"No."

"Okay. Just asking."

Polly, staring out the window, wondered, How do they do it? She could no more go from rage to laughter, from anger to conversation, that way than she could—than she could *fly*, the way a cock pheasant now flew in front of them, a burst of glorious color.

"Isn't he beautiful?" said Mrs. Lewis. But Polly didn't answer and Rusty hadn't seen him.

Chapter four

Polly and Rusty went to the same school, and their classes began at the same time, and a good part of the year they biked the mile and a half there and back, but they never went together. Rusty left early, to meet his friends and play some seasonal game in the yard or in the field behind the school. It would be baseball until the World Series was over, and then they'd switch to basketball. In the olden days, Polly had always stopped by Kate's house and they'd gone on together, chattering away. How had they always found so much to say to each other? What had they talked *about*?

When they'd first talked of California, Kate had said she wouldn't be moving until the end of August, but as it turned out they left toward the end of July. So weeks had gone by now during which Kate had not written and Polly had mostly done things either by herself or with Gram or her parents. She didn't mind doing some things alone. Riding Blondel across pastures, through the woods, going at their own pace—that was fine. She could stop when she wanted to, think about things. Dream.

But what had she and Kate *said* to each other, all the time, all those years?

This morning it had been cold enough for a fire in the wood stove, a fire that Gram would presently let go out as the September day warmed up. Polly, wearing what she'd worn last year on the first day of school, and a woolen cardigan that she'd have tied by the arms around her waist by the time she biked home in the afternoon, left with a wave for Gram, Mom, and Dad, all of whom were standing on the porch to see her off. They'd done it for Rusty, too.

Polly flew downhill, one-handed, eating an apple. The juice sprang at her teeth. One of the sweet, tart, nippy, gnarled apples from their own orchard that had gone so long untended that Mr. Lewis said it might as well be a field of wild apple trees and the fruit from them wildings. They made, these semiwildings, marvelous pie and cider, even if the cider had an occasional worm mashed up in the press. Mr. Ingalls, the farmer who used their pasture for grazing his cattle, said cider wasn't worth the drinking that hadn't had a worm or two or three go through the press.

Polly tossed the core into some bushes, where a raccoon or something would soon find it, and sped on.

No, it wasn't bad, pedaling along on her own this way. A little pang as she passed Kate's house, now lived in by an old couple named Johnstone. But she supposed she was missing Kate less as time went on and no letter came, and the distance between here and California, between her and the girl who had been her best friend, seemed greater with each day that passed.

Just the same, it was sort of sad.

It had rained the night before, and there were several appealing puddles on the road. When she'd been little, she'd loved to spot a nice-sized puddle well ahead, get up to a good—it had to be a *really* good—speed and drive through the center, sending up a wave of water on either side as she sailed through. A person could do this without getting a drop on herself. Of course, she was old for that sort of thing now.

She thought this, saw a pool like a shallow shimmering lake in a wide depression in the road, and began to pedal furiously. The wind flowed against her face, fanned her short hair like a flag as she shot through a wall of water, emerging on the other side with a yelp of joy. As she skimmed around the side of the school building where there was parking for bikes, she saw Consuela arriving, sitting beside her mother in their blue Mercedes. ("There's a woman who knows how to fill her life with splendid rubbish," Mr. Lewis had said. Moya did have lots of gorgeous expensive things that she didn't bother to take care of. The Mercedes might have been a jazzy sports car, but it was dusty and had had one crumpled fender for ages.)

"Hi!" Polly shouted, and Moya, waving, said, "Come over here, Polly. Let me look at you."

Polly trotted to the curb and stood smiling, pushing her hair back. "Look at me?"

"I've decided to paint you. Oh my, if only there were some way of getting you to remain in this state of— Why *are* you so exuberant?"

"Exuberant?"

"You gleam with high spirits. I didn't know young people felt that way about getting to school. I seem to remember hating the first day. What am I saying, *seem*? I definitely loathed it. Used to throw up, regularly, on the first morning."

"That's a shame," said Polly, as if it were still going on. She glanced at Consuela, who seemed composed enough. Consuela always seemed to *wait* while people talked. As if she was very polite but was waiting for silence to fall.

Polly was not going to be shamed into muteness. There was nothing *wrong* in talking, and Moya had *asked* her something. What had she asked? Oh, yes—

"It isn't school, really. I mean, I like school and all. But I just feel good. I feel marvelous. I think it's the weather. We had a fire in the wood stove this morning. It smelled marvelous. I love it when the new season is getting ready to shove the old season out the door."

"What a darling way to put it."

"Gram did, actually."

"I shall just have to try to remember how you look at this moment. That is," she went on confidently, "if you'll agree to pose for me. How about it?"

"I think it'd be super. Hey, there's the bell. Coming, Con—Consuela?"

The year before, they'd had a young man teacher. Mr. Richmond. He'd been great. Kate and lots of the other girls tingled for him. That was what Kate had said, anyway. Kate, when she'd decided to be boy-crazy (because Betty Sackett talked her into it), had also tingled for Arnie Shawl. Arnie was just about the nicest boy in school, maybe in the whole town, but Polly hadn't got around to tingling for boys or young male teachers. It was her opinion that Kate hadn't, either, but had just decided she ought to because of going to Betty Sackett's parties and playing games where people went into closets and kissed each other. Or said they did. Polly wasn't even sure of that, the whole idea seemed so dumb.

Now Mr. Richmond, coming down the hall, said, "Hi, Polly-o. Have a good summer?"

Polly looked at him curiously. He was different—he was— "Mr. Richmond! You've got a beard!"

The young man patted his chin. "I certainly have. You'd think someone could have pointed it out to me before this. I'm obliged, Polly."

Polly giggled. "This is Consuela Christina Machado, Mr. Richmond."

"Oh, yes. I've heard of Consuela and her mother. How do you do, Consuela."

"I'm well," said Consuela. "And it is nice to meet you, Mr. Richmond."

Most people looked a little surprised when Consuela first talked to them. She was so formal. Mr. Richmond said, "Well. Well, nice to see you both. Have a good day."

Polly looked after him. "My father hates that expression."

"What expression?"

"Have a good day."

"What's wrong with it?"

"Nothing, I guess, except too many people say it. You mean you haven't noticed?"

"No."

"But everybody says it to everybody all the time. They put it on their bumper stickers and my father says the last time he went to a funeral everybody but the corpse said have a good day as they were leaving the cemetery. He says he's trying to work up the nerve to punch the next person who says it to him. But Gram says he'd be punching the mailman and the plumber and the carpenter and the carpenter's helper and half the people on the faculty—"

She stopped. Consuela clearly had no idea what she was talking about. Was it just the language barrier, *just* the fact that Connie—Consuela—*thought* in Spanish, even though she spoke English with such a pretty accent and very well most of the time? Gram, at any rate, said she imagined Consuela thought in Spanish and no doubt always would. And it seemed that until you thought in the language you were speaking, you never got its real sense. She wondered if Consuela dreamed in Spanish, too.

She wondered, too, if it wasn't that Consuela didn't pay attention to what went on around her. Wasn't interested. In anything. In anyone. Anyone in Vermont, that was.

This year's teacher was Mrs. Hinshaw. Since the village was so small, it didn't matter which class you were in, you still knew all the teachers and they knew all the children.

Only Consuela was new, was strange. Polly wasn't sure she'd like being in that position. She wondered if today was the first day of school in California. Not that *Kate* would be nervous, the way Consuela probably was. Only, was she? You couldn't tell how Consuela was reacting. There she sat at her desk, her really beautiful face quite still, long black hair lying like a scarf down her straight back, hands folded. Polly, who was usually restless as a water spider—anyway, that's what her grandmother said—could not in any way understand how a person could be so quiet. Practically like a statue.

Mrs. Hinshaw walked to the desk where statuelike Consuela was sitting and said, "I'm sorry not to have had a chance to meet you before, Connie. I just got back from my vacation yesterday. But welcome to our town and to our class. Class, this is Consuela Christina Machado. I think it would be nice if each of you stood in turn and gave your name. Not that you'll be able to remember them all at once, Connie, but it will be a start. We'll begin at the left-hand corner and go across the room and then backward and forward across each row of desks—I'll explain about these desks in a little while. All right, Calvin Aiken, do you wish to begin?"

Cal, scowling, said his name without standing. That was something Mr. Richmond, even if he'd suggested that they stand, would just have let pass. Mr. Richmond would've given Cal a meaningful look and then waited to see if the next kid, Faith Jennings in this case, wanted to follow his suggestion. But Mrs. Hinshaw, while she was an okay lady in most ways, was strict about having all her suggestions followed, even if they didn't matter much. Anyway, thought Polly, as Faith stood and said her name, and then Betty Sackett stood and said hers—fondly and clearly—anyway, it wouldn't seem that it would matter if you stood or not. But Mrs. Hinshaw, with a nod to Faith and Betty, turned back to Cal.

"Cal, I feel it would be politer if you stood while introducing yourself."

Cal shambled to his feet and stood.

"Well?" said Mrs. Hinshaw.

"Well what?" Cal was a rude boy and always had been. Mrs. Lewis said that Mr. and Mrs. Aiken, his parents, said they believed in waiting for their children to be *motivated* to be polite. They didn't want to force them. They had five and so far none of them had been motivated.

"Calvin," said Mrs. Hinshaw, "you have been asked to stand and give your name."

"I already gave it, and now I'm standing."

Buzz Nickerson snorted, then looked around, pretending to wonder who'd done it.

"I see," said Mrs. Hinshaw. "Very well, Calvin. Now you may sit."

So Calvin and Mrs. Hinshaw had laid the groundwork, on the first day in the first hour, for one of those teacher-pupil enmities that could last the whole year.

Gram and her own parents insisted on teaching her and Rusty manners. Not that Rusty was a quick study, but he was better than Cal Aiken. "Can't wait for you to be motivated," Mr. Lewis said. "It'd probably take too long and I'd be too old to reap the benefits." And Gram held that it would be as unnatural for a child to be motivated to be polite as to be motivated to eat the proper food or take baths. Of course Rusty was resisting them. He was rude as often as he thought he could get away with it, and he put up what Mr. Lewis called a truly heroic stand against baths. . . .

"Polly Lewis?"

Polly jumped to her feet. "Sorry, Mrs. Hinshaw. I was thinking. I'm Polly Lewis," she said, smiling at Consuela, who was sitting as if frozen, staring straight ahead. Polly thought she probably hadn't heard a single name or looked

at a single face. She hoped Mrs. Hinshaw wouldn't—
But Mrs. Hinshaw did.

"And now, Connie," she said. "Suppose you stand and tell us a little about yourself, about your own country?"

For a moment, Polly thought Consuela would refuse. Or, worse, not even be able to get out words of refusal. But after what seemed ages, Consuela, her olive skin darkly flushed, got to her feet, and still staring ahead, as if trying to think herself right out of the room, said, "My name is Consuela Christina Machado." She stopped, went on. "My country, Mexico" (she pronounced it Meh-hee-ko) "is—is very beautiful. The language, Español, are different—is different to here. And our clotheses, too. Those are different. More gayer." She stopped again, biting her lip. Polly felt a rush of protective embarrassment for this girl she scarcely considered a friend, only a horse sharer. Even Consuela's practically perfect English was deserting her, and her accent seemed stronger than usual.

In the waiting silence, as Mrs. Hinshaw opened her lips to let, Polly was sure, Connie off the hook, Betty Sackett could be heard muttering to Faith, "*Clotheses*, for goodness' sakes. And look at her skin. I bet she's colored. . . ."

"Betty!" Mrs. Hinshaw was furious. "You apologize this moment—"

But Consuela turned to where Betty was sitting and for the first time focused her eyes *on* something, in this case Betty's flushed face. Betty had not intended to be heard and was angry at everybody but herself because she had been.

"I do not ask an apology for that," said Consuela, in control of the language once again. "My grandmother is Indian. I guess *you*—I do not recall your name—I guess

38

you think you were making an insult. My grandmother is Indian and beautiful and she has manners. I do not want an apology for my skin color."

She sat down.

"Whew," said Arnie Shawl. "She's great."

Consuela affected not to hear, but Polly turned right around in her seat to look at Betty, who, sure enough, was scowling like mad. Betty wouldn't think for a moment that *she'd* done anything wrong. She'd be blaming her situation on Mrs. Hinshaw, on Consuela, on maybe even Consuela's grandmother. But never on herself. Besides, she had a case on Arnie.

It was a pretty awful beginning of the first day of school, and Polly couldn't help wishing that Mr. Richmond had been teaching the class that saw Consuela Christina Machado into her first American school.

Chapter five

"Bless us, oh Lord, and these thy gifts—"

"Amen," said Polly. "Mrs. Hinshaw says—Oh, hadn't you finished, Gram?" she asked, at her father's expression.

"I had thought to go on, but I suppose we can stop there," said her grandmother.

"No, please. Honestly. Sometimes you finish up there."

"Rusty does. I always like to finish the whole blessing. It's a nice one, and not too long."

"Say it, Gram," Rusty put in. "I'm getting hungry."

"Perhaps," said Mr. Lewis, "we should just eliminate the practice of saying grace before our evening meals."

"No!" said Rusty and Polly together.

"You appear unanimous in that, and yet night after night one of you interrupts. Saying grace is not just a mumbling of words. It's supposed to be a moment—only a moment, mind—of sincere reflectiveness, and thankfulness. If you can't give it even that moment, what is the point of saying it?"

Polly and Rusty looked at each other, at their parents and their grandmother. Daddy's right, Polly thought. Such a little moment. And such a lot to be thankful for. She wondered why it was hard to remember to be thankful.

40

"I think we should keep saying it," said Rusty. "I don't mind going hungry."

"That's the spirit that martyrs were made of," his mother observed in a dry tone.

"Ah, gee, Mom—"

Old Mrs. Lewis folded her hands again, bringing silence. "Bless us, oh Lord, and these thy gifts, which we are about to receive, through Christ, our Lord. Amen."

"Dig in, Rusty," said his father.

Rusty sat back in his chair, arms folded to indicate that he was not going to eat unless pleaded with. As the rest of them went ahead, in a moment he shrugged and picked up his fork.

"Now, what were you saying about Mrs. Hinshaw?" Gram asked Polly.

"Gram, I'm sorry about—"

"Dearie, the point has been made, I think. Let's move along to the next subject."

Polly, like Rusty, debated whether to sulk, decided against it. "Well, what she says is that by coincidence we're going to study Latin America for the first two months. The coincidence is Consuela being with us and so she can tell us a lot about Mexico. Except she got so upset trying even to say a little about it that I don't know."

"Why did she get upset?"

"Pass the potatoes," said Rusty.

"Please," said his mother.

"Okay, you can have them first."

"Because she got nervous," said Polly. "Because, probably, she's shy, like you said."

"*As* I said," said Mr. Lewis.

41

"I thought it was Gram said it. Anyway, she didn't have such a marvelous first day, I guess. I mean, she didn't even come back after lunch."

"What do you mean, didn't come back?" Anna Lewis asked. "You have lunch at school."

"But Connie—Consuela—just walked out of the building and went home. I suppose she went home. Anyway, she wasn't there this afternoon."

"That poor child," said Gram. "I wish there were some way we could help her."

"You could ask her and her mother for supper," Polly pointed out. "I mean, she rides Blondel, but she's never been inside the house. Only the barn."

"Have you asked her?"

"Well, Gram. Of course I have. But she always just says she has to get home. But I think that if once she and her mother came here, got *invited*, she'd feel she could come in other times, see? I think she's the sort who has to have an invitation. She's formal, you know."

"Her mother certainly isn't," said Anna Lewis.

"Well, but Consuela *is*, so if you'd—"

"All right," said Mrs. Lewis. "I'll call Ms. O'Shea tomorrow and ask them for Friday."

"She wants you to call her Moya."

"I'll try."

"Do you know," Polly went on, "this year we have desks. Instead of the open classroom. They're in rows, and we have to sit at them and not wander around during lessons. It's a new method they're trying in school."

"Hardly new," said Mr. Lewis. "Just to you."

"That's what Mrs. Hinshaw said."

That morning, when Consuela had sat down, trembling a little after telling Betty Sackett off, Mrs. Hinshaw had looked as if she might say some words to Betty herself, but then had changed her mind.

"About these desks," she'd said. "It's the first time we're trying this method in our school and we're hoping it will result in a bit more—concentration, on everybody's part. You will please remain at your desks unless for some reason you either need or are asked to leave them—"

"You mean we gotta hold up our hands if we gotta go to the ca— the bathroom?" Buzz Nickerson said with a snigger.

"No, Buzz. That will not be necessary. But in general, we're hoping that less random wandering about the room will result in better schoolwork. Any of you who've read *Tom Sawyer*—how many have, by the way?"

All the hands in the room went up, except Buzz's.

"It was on the summer reading list, Buzz."

"Mr. Richmond said we didn't hafta read anything on that list. Just we could if we wanted to. I didn't want to."

"What did you read from the list?"

"Nothing. I looked at it and decided I didn't want to read anything on it. I hate reading."

Mrs. Hinshaw looked at him for a moment, then returned to the matter of the desks. "As I was saying, anybody who's read *Tom Sawyer* knows that this is scarcely a new system in classrooms. Just new to all of you. We'll try it for a year throughout the school and see how it works."

"In *Tom Sawyer*," Cal Aiken said, "he got walloped by the teacher. Are you going to wallop us?"

"Oh, for heaven's sakes. No, you are not going to be walloped. Now, by an interesting coincidence, we are going to study Latin America for the first two months of this term."

"What's an interesting coincidence about it?" Buzz asked.

"That should be obvious. We have the pleasure of a Mexican student's presence in our class, and should be able to learn much from her—"

Consuela's lips whitened, but Mrs. Hinshaw didn't call on her again that morning, and when the lunch period was over, Consuela was gone. Polly had looked for her in the yard where they ate the lunches they brought from home, but supposed she hadn't looked very hard. She'd eaten with Faith and Sandra and then played jacks with them until the bell rang. Mrs. Hinshaw had gone out, probably to the principal's office, but hadn't said anything about Connie when she came back.

When supper was over, Mr. Lewis washed the dishes and Rusty dried them. To his annoyance, Rusty had been promoted from someone considered too unreliable to handle dishes to someone permitted to dry them but please be careful. The first night, he'd dropped a salad plate and broken it. On purpose, Polly was pretty sure. If so, the scheme hadn't worked, because he'd just been asked to be more careful if possible, and hadn't dropped one since. They didn't use the dishwasher anymore because it was wasteful of water. Waste of water, of electricity, of paper, of fuel, of food . . . of about anything except time (Mr. Lewis said that occasional waste of time was good for the soul) was frowned upon in Polly's family. Gram had once said that until the energy crisis came ("Which," she'd added, "*we* all saw coming a good long time ago"), the Lewises had been considered, by some people, stingy. Now they were looked on as good conservationists. Polly thought that her brother, fending off baths with such vigor, was the best water conserver of them all.

While Mr. Lewis and Rusty were at the sink, Polly swept the kitchen floor, Gram set the table for breakfast, and Mrs. Lewis sat in the rocker by the wood stove, smiling at so much industry in which she was taking no part. Everyone got a turn to sit in the rocker and look on once every five nights. Mrs. Lewis said that watching others work when you didn't have to was also good for the soul.

When that was done, they went out on the lawn to throw the Frisbee back and forth. Summer evenings, they sat on the porch off the kitchen, talking and dreaming as the dark came on, but now there was a current of autumn in the twilight air and it was better to do something lively.

"Hah!" shouted Mr. Lewis, as the disc shot from his wife to his mother to Polly. "Tinker to Evers to Chance!"

"What's that mean, Daddy?" Polly asked.

"Don't stop the game, Polly-o! We've got a volley going! Tinker to Evers to Chance—the most famous play ever made in baseball—"

"Oh," said Polly. "Baseball." She turned her wrist in, spun the Frisbee to her mother, who caught it, sent it spinning to Rusty, who sent it on to Gram, who snatched it with a leap in the air.

"Hey, Gram," Rusty said admiringly. "That's neat—"

As Gram prepared to shoot, the telephone in the

kitchen rang and the Frisbee wobbled out of her grasp into the bushes.

"Darn," she said.

"I'll get it," Polly offered. "Keep playing."

But they all followed her in.

"Getting dark anyway," said Anna Lewis, pushing back her hair and laughing. "That was fun."

"Mom," said Polly, turning from the phone. "It's for you. Or for Daddy. Either one. It's Mrs.—I mean, Ms.—its Moya."

"Oh?" Anna Lewis took the telephone, said hello and then listened for a while. "Well, of course," she said at length. "Any time you say. No, we aren't doing anything special right now. . . . Well, of course we would, but won't Consuela— I see. . . . Well, we'll see you in a few minutes, then." She hung up. "Moya O'Shea. She seems quite upset about Connie. Consuela. Says she has no one to talk to, so could she talk to us. What could I say?"

"Why shouldn't she talk to us?" Polly demanded.

"I didn't mean that the way it sounded. I meant, I don't see what help we can be."

"Daddy can. He can be a help."

"You, Polly, are too prefeminist to be true."

"What's that?" Rusty asked. "Prefeminist?"

"A term used for females who persist in thinking men are superior to women in all ways."

"Why shouldn't they think that?" Rusty asked, and grinned when his grandmother said, "Rusty, go split some wood or something, before I bop you one."

"I only meant," Polly explained, "that Daddy is a teacher, so he can figure out what to do about somebody

46

running away from school."

"I don't quite follow your reasoning," said Mr. Lewis. "However. Is she bringing Consuela with her?" he asked his wife.

"No. Consuela's in her room. She's been there since she got home, only a couple of hours ago. Won't talk, won't eat. Ms. O'Shea—Moya, darn it, *Moya*—doesn't even know where she's been all afternoon."

Struck with an idea, Polly got up and went out to the barn. When she got back, she said, "Consuela's been riding Blondel."

"Are you sure?"

"Sure, I'm sure. She always puts the saddle back on the rack facing frontward, so I'll know he's been ridden." The arrangement she and Consuela had come to was that if Polly wanted her horse to herself, she'd leave a note on the saddle. If there was no note, Connie was free to ride him. It was good for Blondel to be taken out every day, and even though she'd been praised for unselfishly sharing her horse, Polly knew she wasn't as unselfish as she was letting people think she was. She just didn't want to ride alone, day after day, the way she used to. Anyway, Kate used to ride with her a couple of times a week, but Consuela had only ridden double that one night when they'd gone to the Fair. She supposed she ought to point this out to people, so they wouldn't go on calling her unselfish. On the other hand, maybe she was setting a good example for Rusty, who didn't have an unselfish bone in his body. . . .

"I don't think I'll take part in this discussion," said Gram.

"She said she wanted to consult all of us," Anna Lewis

said. "She really did sound frightfully upset. I didn't think anything could upset her. Always seems so in command, doesn't she?"

"I'm gonna go split some wood," Rusty announced, disappearing through the door to the shed, trailed by Okie. As they went, the lights of Moya O'Shea's car angled into the driveway and went off.

There was no way, apparently, for her not to look marvelous. You could tell she was nervous, Polly thought, but rushing into the kitchen, eyes wide, faintly fragrant of something delicious, with black narrow slacks and a big loosely knit purple sweater, dark hair tied at the back, tumbling out here and there in wisps and curls, she looked to Polly like an actress acting nervous, not a real person being nervous.

But her voice shook as she said, "This is so very very good of you—I simply hadn't a notion where to turn or what to do—do you know that Connie simply walked out of school on her first day at lunchtime and didn't go back and I don't know where she did go—they tried to call me from the school but I was out all afternoon and she says she isn't going back *ever*, and what am I going to do?" She put one hand to her forehead, as if her head ached.

"Let's go in and sit down," Anna Lewis said, leading the way to the living room. "There's one thing we can settle. Polly says Consuela was riding Blondel this afternoon."

"Oh?" said Moya, spinning around. "How do you know? Were you with her?"

"No. We have this system with the saddle."

Moya didn't ask what the system was. "All *I* know is that she came in around five o'clock and said she wasn't going back to school and didn't want any dinner. I never force Connie to eat, and she often skips dinner. To punish me, I think."

"For what?" Gram asked.

"Oh, dear. I don't know. Maybe I know. I think, don't you, that some people are designed by *nature* to be good parents. All of you, for example. Clearly *made* for parenthood. But some people simply shouldn't be allowed to have children, and I'm one of them. I *try* to be a proper mother, and goodness knows I love her. But I don't know. Work keeps interfering, for one thing. And then, Connie's so resentful of the divorce—"

"Why do you call her Connie?" Anna Lewis asked. "She wants to be called Consuela."

"What she *wants*, actually, is to be called Consuela Christina. That's what they call her in Guadalajara. Her father calls her Consuela Christina, and all the aunts and grandparents and servants. . . ."

"But then why—"

"What I'm *trying* to do is wean her away from Mexico. Calling her Consuela keeps her so in mind of Guadalajara and all she's left behind, including being reared to be a *doll*, a beautiful nothing, a—a *frippery*. *Connie* sounds so *un*-Mexican. Now look, I adore Mexico. I don't want you to misunderstand. But their ideas about rearing girl children are *not* mine, and she is my daughter. But I don't know," she said again. "Maybe I was wrong to bring her up here. She's miserable. She misses her father, and Favorita—that's an aunt she adores—and El Cometo, that's her horse—and truth to tell I'm not sure which of them all she misses most. Maybe mostly just Mexico. She's horribly homesick—such a painful emotion and I

49

do sympathize, but what am I to do? I'm not much happier myself and we do grate on each other something awful. If only she had a friend—Polly, *why* can't you be her friend?"

"I am her friend. I'm just not sure she's mine. Mostly she wants to ride Blondel, I guess. She's *very* polite and takes good care of him and it's good for him to be ridden every day. . . ." She was babbling, not wanting to give the impression, which she had herself, that Consuela was interested in her only for her horse.

"I've *offered* to get her a horse of her own, but no. She just refuses . . . no explanation. Just a straight no thanks . . ."

("Not that you aren't perfectly welcome to Blondel," Polly had said one day to Consuela, "but wouldn't you like to have a horse of your own? Didn't you have one, in Texas?"

"El Cometo," Consuela had said softly. "He came up with us from Mexico. Now he's back in Guadalajara on the ranch." She'd stopped, looking across the pasture toward the hills. Polly, who had learned to wait out Consuela's silences, if they didn't last *too* long, waited. "Do you think," Consuela resumed at last, "that he'll remember me, when I go down for Christmas?"

"Of course. You mean you'd feel disloyal, owning another horse? You wouldn't have to tell him, you know."

"It isn't that." Consuela ran her hand down Blondel's neck. He pawed the ground lightly, turned his head and nibbled at her hair. "It's— She'd get me something expensive. El Cometo is an old cow pony who can't work with the cattle anymore.")

Polly wondered whether to repeat this conversation

now to Moya, decided against it.

"Then I take it," Mr. Lewis was saying, "that you haven't talked with Consuela about what happened today at all?"

"But I *told* you. All she said was she wasn't going back to school and then went into her room and closed the door. Isn't there some sort of law? I mean, isn't she *required* to go? In the general way, I don't think much of schools, or even of education, come to that. But there are some *basics* that people should know, wouldn't you say?"

"As a teacher myself," said Mr. Lewis, "I don't share your view of education—"

"Oh, dear me. Dear *me*. Can you *ever* forgive me?"

"Easily," said Mr. Lewis. "As to Consuela—quite a few children threaten, for one reason or another, never to go to school again. They're hurt, or frightened, or feel inadequate. Not going back is the only solution they can think of."

"What solution do you see?" Moya demanded.

"Leave her alone for a day or two. Don't tell her she must go back, and don't threaten—"

"Goodness, I never do that. I'm more the pleading type."

"Well." Mr. Lewis studied his guest. Polly could tell he wasn't much taken with Moya. "The other thing you could do, and should, I think, is go to Mrs. Hinshaw and ask her not to call on your daughter in class. Polly tells us that Consuela got extremely nervous at being called on. If she were reassured on this point, I think in a few days she'd go back to school on her own. Perhaps Polly, if she wanted to, could ride up to your house one afternoon and just talk with Consuela. Not about anything in

51

particular. Just talk. Polly's good at that."

"Okay by me," said Polly. "She may not want to—"

"Oh, but I'm sure she *will*," Moya said. "She's very fond of you, Polly." She tipped her head, studying Polly's face. "Did this child tell you that I want to paint her? Ordinarily I don't paint children. They're so uninteresting. But this morning outside the school Polly simply swept into the yard on her bicycle with an expression of perfectly *fierce* joy. Quite bewitching, if I can recapture it. Are you frequently fiercely joyful, Polly?"

"Well, gee . . ."

"Never mind. You come up for sittings, and *I'll* remember the expression. It's practically painted in my head now. Oh, this Consuela thing—it's so hard to *cope*. I have so much to *do* and only one lifetime, and one day, one day if I'm right in my vision, I shall paint something strange and beautiful that will change the world. Oh, yes . . . one day, one day. But if I'm to be constantly interrupted with visits to *teachers* . . . I don't suppose you—" She looked at Anna Lewis doubtfully.

"No," said Polly's mother. "I'm afraid it's something you'll have to attend to yourself. Mrs. Hinshaw would not appreciate suggestions from me."

"I see. Well, there's no help for it. I'll do what you say, and believe me, I can't thank you enough, all of you. It's—it's hard, sometimes, being alone with no one to turn to. That's the worst part of divorce, suddenly having no one to turn to. Better, probably, not to marry to begin with—"

When she'd gone, the Lewises sat in silence for a while and then Mr. Lewis said, "Why do you suppose she brought the girl up with her at all?"

"She said she wanted to prevent her from being turned into a Mexican doll."

"So she did. Maybe she means it. But do you realize that she managed to say she regretted both marrying *and* having a child?"

"She didn't quite say that," Anna Lewis protested.

"All but. It's no wonder the girl wanders around looking lost. She is lost. A father in Texas and a mother in a vision of greatness."

"What's their house like, Polly?" Gram asked suddenly.

Polly looked around her own living room. Large, well used, always a little untidy. There were books on tables and even on the floor in spite of a wall of bookcases. A big old Oriental rug, down cushions on chairs and sofas that only got fluffed up once a week. Pictures on the wall, usually a little crooked. Moya had looked at the pictures but had made no comment on them. There was a fire laid in the hearth but it hadn't been lit this year yet. On the mantel was a pretty little French clock, and against one wall a piano with music open on the rack. A nice room, and Polly loved it. But it wasn't exciting. Moya's house was the grandest, the strangest she ever could imagine. The living room was huge and high ceilinged with one sloping wall of glass, a tremendous fireplace, lots of low bright squashy furniture and scatter rugs and all sorts of odd lovely things lying about any whichway. There was a bowlful of unset jewels, like a pirate's treasure. Amethysts, crystals, cats' eyes and tourmalines and topazes, maybe a pound or two of them, all glittering together in a careless mound. Moya didn't wear jewelry, but sometimes she'd put her hands in this bowl of brilliants and just turn them around, watching them flash. She'd let Polly do that. There was a lemon tree taller than Polly, and a big terrarium with lots of frondy plants and a big piece of petrified wood and a salamander that at first she'd thought was carved but then it had moved its tail. From the ceiling hung a mobile of huge insects made of colored glass and hammered silver. There was a large bronze statue of a dancer. Moya said it was a dancer. To Polly it looked like a top. Moya had made the mobile and the bronze dancer herself, and she'd made the terrarium. Her easel and painting stuff were over in one corner of the room, under the slanting glass wall. There was a staircase winding up to the gallery where the bedrooms were, Moya's and Consuela's, with a bathroom between. Those rooms were small. Under the gallery were stacked hundreds of canvases, and on all the walls except the glass one hung paintings by Moya O'Shea. Bursting gardens and clouds and storms and strange animal-insect-bird forms. Houses that weren't broken down but looked empty. Landscapes that gave the feeling that either the sun was shining and it was just about to rain, or it was raining and the sun was just about to come out.

When Polly had been small, one of her favorite presents to get was a coloring book. She could still remember the feeling of excitement when she'd tear off the gift wrapping and find a big book with outlines of animals and trees, houses and fields, on the pages. A box of waxy, sharp-smelling crayons to go with it. Crayons and coloring books were long past, of course, but she still found the day that Mrs. Farquhar, the county art teacher, came to their school the one she most looked forward to. To be an artist. That would be a wonderful thing. Maybe, as Moya said, if a person was going to be an artist, she should not be a mother too. Poor Consuela. To think that when she first came, I thought she must be maybe the luckiest person in the world, to have a gorgeous famous artist for a mother. Feeling fond, a bit guilty for having wavered about them even for a second, Polly looked at her parents, at her dear Gram. Talk about being lucky—

"It's a marvelous house," she said. "But not like ours."

The next day Consuela came into the classroom in the morning and took her place without a word. Polly thought she was brave. Her mother wouldn't have had time to talk to Mrs. Hinshaw yet, so Consuela had done this on her own. Polly wasn't sure she'd have been able to, in Guadalajara, Mexico.

But on that day, and for many days following, Consuela didn't talk to anyone, not even to Polly. She stopped riding Blondel. Mrs. Hinshaw did not ask her anything in class again, and she disappeared at noon with her lunchbox, looking as if she wanted to be alone. So people let her alone, Polly included.

Chapter six

In their study of Latin America, said Mrs. Hinshaw, one of the most interesting projects they had before them was to make maps.

"Maps of what?" Buzz Nickerson groaned.

"Let's all guess," Arnie Shawl suggested. "Asia, I betcha."

"Boy, you're funny as a cage of monkeys, I don't think," said Buzz.

"My first compliment today," Arnie said happily. "I'm going to put it down in this little notebook I have for putting in the compliments I get—"

"All right," said Mrs. Hinshaw. "You're both quite witty, but time is passing." She pulled down a large map in front of the blackboard. It showed North and South America. Polly was surprised to find that South America was not directly underneath, but sort of bulged over to the east. The things you did learn in school.

"Now, there is one habit we shall all have to get over," Mrs. Hinshaw went on, "and that is calling our country, that is, the United States, America. As if there were no others. There's North America, which consists of the United States, including Alaska, as well as Canada on our northern border and Mexico on our southern border. . . ." She made such a point of not looking at Connie that everybody else did. Polly decided that at some time in the past few days Moya must have had the talk with the teacher that she said would be such an interruption to her work. "And beneath that," Mrs. Hinshaw continued, "in a kind of link between North and South America, we have Central America, and then South America. So you can see that we have no reason to call ourselves 'Americans' in the exclusive way that we do—"

"My father says all those countries are troublemakers," said Buzz. "He says they're banana republics. What's a banana republic, Mrs. Hinshaw?"

"Oh, Buzz." Mrs. Hinshaw sighed. "A so-called banana republic is any one of the Central American countries or Caribbean islands which, in fact, does export bananas. It's a term of insult. It does not refer to all of Latin America—"

"My old man says all those countries down there are dictatorships. They don't have any freedoms, like we have. He says they're all run by a bunch of lousy dictators."

This time Mrs. Hinshaw did glance at Consuela who, to everyone's astonishment, said, "My father says the same thing." She lapsed into silence again.

After a moment, Mrs. Hinshaw resumed. "To a certain—well, to a great extent, this is true. But it is not a reason for us not to study these countries. The more we try to understand the people of countries which have fallen under dictatorships, try to find out what steps they may be taking toward gaining their own freedom of expression, their right to live as individuals, the better we'll understand them. And maybe we'll also come to understand ourselves, our own country, better. Now, look at this map and then each of you decide which country you wish to do a map of. After that, we'll each study our country carefully. Its history, agriculture, climate, the way the people live, the politics. Oh, I think you're going to find this very interesting. Yes, Buzz? What is it?"

"I'm gonna do America. I mean, the United States."

"Buzz! We are about to study *Latin* America, not—"

"But you got North America there on the map."

"That was to show you the western hemisphere, to give you an idea of the relative positions and sizes of the various countries. You may not do a map of the United States."

"Okay, then I take Panama. It's the smallest."

"I see. What about the rest of you?"

Various pupils announced their choices. Some seemed interested, some bored, but that was how it always was in school. Polly, who was never bored by anything, looked at Betty. It was funny how anyone pretty could look so dull, but Betty managed. She said she'd take Ecuador for goodness' sakes. That was almost as small as Panama. Polly opted for Brazil because it was biggest. She could see her map forming in her mind. Mrs. Hinshaw was handing out some big sheets of drawing paper, but Polly had already decided to use something much better than that. She'd get a roll of brown wrapping paper and make a *really* big map. She'd draw the outline and put in the cities and lakes and mountains as Mrs. Hinshaw had suggested, but she was also going to look up all the kinds of plants and animals they had down there and she'd draw them in, too, in the parts of the country they belonged to, and then she'd color the whole thing with her pastel crayons.

"You can work on this project at home," Mrs. Hinshaw said. "I'll consider it your homework in everything but arithmetic for the next month. That will include, of course, diligent study about the country itself, not just drawing a map. You will submit a paper to go with your map, and on Parents' Night in October we'll display the maps and the papers. How does that sound?"

"Sounds dandy to me," said Polly, earning a grateful smile from Mrs. Hinshaw. She always, in every class, ended up—or even started out—by being teacher's pet. It wasn't her fault, and except for people like Betty nobody held it against her. Her problem was that she really liked school, and her father said that no teacher can resist a student who likes school. Arnie Shawl ran her a close second in this matter, and since nobody ever criticized Arnie, she was sort of protected by his being another teacher's pet.

The bell rang, and they took their lunch boxes, or brown paper bags, out of their desks. Polly enjoyed having a desk. You could work on the lid, and keep your books and pencil box and lunch inside, and so far it had seemed to keep the class more in order than in other years when they'd been free to wander all around and sit on the floor and even ignore the teacher if they wanted to. Buzz and some of the others said it was like being in jail, but that was because they had to pay more attention than they wanted to.

Still, they were not used to desks, and by lunchtime everybody was restless, scuffling their feet, turning around to look out the windows, making faces at each other.

Mrs. Hinshaw, as the morning drew on, pretended not to notice signs of fidgets. She didn't say anything, either, when late in the morning someone too itchy to sit still just got up and walked around before sitting down again. In the whole class Consuela was the only one who simply sat, hands folded quietly on her desk, her whole self quiet and unmoving. Polly didn't see how she did it.

Now she took her lunch box and went out into the school yard, but instead of sitting with Faith and Sandra, she looked around to find out where Consuela was, where she'd been going to eat by herself these days. Her father had asked her to find time to ride up to the O'Shea house and talk with Consuela. She hadn't done it yet. Each afternoon she thought she would and each afternoon decided that if she got up there and Consuela just would not talk it would be so embarrassing that neither of them would get over it.

Here, at school, at lunchtime, it would be simpler. If she could find Consuela.

The school was next to the Congregational church. Behind that was an old churchyard. Nobody had been buried in it for a hundred years and some of the thin tombstones were so old that all the markings had been weathered off them. On a sudden thought, Polly walked out of the school yard, around to the back of the church, and sure enough, there was Consuela, sitting on an overturned slab, eating a sandwich.

Polly stepped over the low stone wall and walked between the headstones, as though idly. "Oh, hi!" she said, trying to sound surprised. "Didn't know there was anyone here."

Consuela looked at her and then began to giggle.

"You're funny."

"I guess I am. Mind if I sit with you?"

"No." Consuela moved down the slab, making room. "My mother asked you to be friendly with me, didn't she, that night she said she was going for a ride but really went to your house."

"How do you know she went to our house?"

"I heard her talking to your mother on the phone."

"Nobody had to ask me to be friendly with you. You just always act as if you don't want to be. Well, nearly always. You aren't riding Blondel anymore, are you?"

Consuela nibbled a piece of celery. "Sometimes I get so I don't want to talk to anybody or see anybody."

Sometimes? Polly thought. "You don't have to talk to Blondel. I do, all the time, of course, but he doesn't insist on it."

"I guess I'm not very—gracious. You were so nice about letting me ride him and then I just stopped without saying anything—" She broke off, but this time Polly waited. If Consuela wanted to say something more, fine. If she didn't, that was okay, too.

It was a lovely day, warm with crisp edges. Over in the hills scarlet and yellow leaves, whole branches of them, were beginning to appear on the trees. The churchyard here was dappled with leaves blown from maples and sycamores in the fields beyond. Polly could see why someone would come here to be peaceful. You wouldn't want to eat your lunch in a *new* graveyard with a lot of shiny marble and crypts and statues and things. But this place seemed so gentle and quiet, so smoothed by all the years and years of wind and snow and rain. No one could be nervous here.

"That first day," Consuela said, looking straight ahead as she so often did when she talked to someone, "that first day in school. That was awful. I thought I really never could come back. What I thought was—" She stopped again.

"That you'd run away to Mexico."

"How did you know?"

Polly lifted her shoulders. "Just guessed."

"Well, I did. I mean, I did think that's what I'd do. But I guess running away isn't as easy as it sounds. I couldn't even figure how to start. Anyway, if I *got* to Guadalajara somehow, they'd only send me back."

"Don't they like you?" Polly blurted.

"They love me. But they—my family abides by arrangements. It's not honorable not to abide by arrangements. The arrangement is I stay with my mother during the school year and go to Mexico at vacation time."

"Don't you mean Texas? Isn't your father in Texas?"

"Oh, he's too busy with the clinic for me to go there. That was one of the reasons for the arrangement. For me to be with my mother, mostly. My father's too busy. He loves me, you know, but the clinic keeps him busy all the time."

"I see."

They sat in silence for a while. Somebody kept the grass mowed in here, but at the edge of the wall and up into the field were the weeds of autumn. Such pretty weeds. Queen Anne's lace, lythrum, chicory, brown-eyed Susans, jewelweed, goldenrod . . . And such pretty cloud formations up above.

"It really is nice here," Polly said lazily. "Aren't you ever going to ride Blondel anymore?"

"Yes, I'd like to. Thank you."

The school bell rang and they stood up, closing their lunch boxes, and walked back together.

That afternoon after school Consuela, who usually took the school bus, rode back to Polly's house on the handlebars of Polly's bike. Taking bridle and saddle from the barn they went across the road to whistle for Blondel, grazing in the meadow with Mr. Ingalls' cattle. He came trotting down the fence line, shaking his head in greeting, prancing a bit. Blondel liked it when the weather began to get cool. He grew foalish. Polly bridled and saddled him, then Consuela, after checking the cinches, mounted lightly.

"Enjoy it," said Polly, patting her pony's nose. "Because pretty soon the deer season begins, and that's the end of riding for you, my fellow. You'll have to go to the village with me and help with the marketing. No woods, do you hear?"

"*Ciao*," said Consuela, leaning the reins against his neck. She started off at a walk.

When Polly was leaving someone, she always turned to wave. Everyone in her family did that. If they were seeing someone off, they waited in case the person turned. "It would be awful," said Gram, "for somebody to look back and find only a closed door. As if they'd already been forgotten."

Consuela never turned. But she always lifted a hand backward and flipped her fingers. It's a funny way to do, thought Polly, but nice. She watched the slim figure sitting so tall and straight on Blondel, walking at first, then breaking into an easy trot. Sure enough, just as they got to the part of the pasture where a rider would disappear around a copse of small firs, the arm went up, the fingers waggled a good-bye motion, and Blondel broke into a canter.

Polly walked slowly back across the road, stopping to watch a turtle coming in the opposite direction. A painted terrapin with orange markings on his shell. His head looked like a green celery knob, and he lunged slowly forward on his thinly webbed feet, long nails gripping the macadam. Why would a turtle decide to cross the road? To get on the other side? What would be on the other side that would not be on the side where he already was? His family? Would a turtle remember that he had a family, much less where he'd last seen the members of it? Something better to eat? But the foraging would be the same on either side. She decided the turtle didn't have anything special in mind. He'd just come to a road and started across it. At the rate he traveled, chances were he wouldn't make it. A car was coming now, down the hill. Polly skipped over, plucked the painted terrapin from the road, and took him to the pasture, since that was where he'd been headed, even if not where he wanted to be, and shoved him carefully under the fence. He'd withdrawn completely at her touch, so she waited awhile, watching. In a few minutes the head emerged warily, the four feet slid out to take a purchase on the grass, the little pointed tail came out and swayed back and forth, and off he went.

Zero miles an hour, thought Polly, and went into the house smiling.

"Consuela's riding Blondel," she said to her grandmother.

"Oh, that's *fine*. Do you think she's feeling better?"

64

"I guess. Where are you going?"

"I thought I'd go upstairs and tint my hair. The gray is beginning to show and somebody might come to the conclusion that this nice licorice color isn't my own. Can't have that. Why?"

"I thought—I was just thinking it's such a nice day, it might be fun to walk up the hay lane and just sit there, looking around. Pretty soon it'll be too cold just to sit on the ground and look. But if you want to do your hair—"

"I should much prefer walking up the hay lane with you. Now," her grandmother said, as they went out the kitchen door and started up the hill, "tell me about school."

Nobody's ever too busy for Rusty and me, Polly thought. Not Gram, not Mom or Daddy. They *always* have time for us.

"We're going to make these maps," she said. "And I've got this idea, Gram, about how I'm going to do mine—"

Chapter seven

One evening Polly was sitting at the kitchen table, her map of Brazil spread out, taking up practically one entire end. She'd got the outline done, and had printed in the names of cities and the larger towns, and drawn the rivers—the great Amazon and its tributaries—and put some cross-hatching for mountains. That had been fun to do, but the best was still to come. Now she was drawing in all the various animals that lived there, and all the plants. Well . . . not *all*. In studying about Brazil for her paper she'd discovered that there were about fifty thousand different species of plants in the rain forests there. Even with a map this big, she wasn't going to be able to fit them all in. And animals! Creatures she'd never even heard of. She'd already drawn a wonderful jaguar, a parrot leaning out of a tree to look at him and a couple of howler monkeys sitting at the top of a strangler fig. She hadn't been able to find a picture of a strangler fig and so had drawn a tree with a vine crawling around it with big fistlike leaves. She'd drawn some figs in the branches. It was more fun, in a way, not to know what something looked like when you wanted to draw it. She had, however, found a picture of a capybara, which was a rat as big as a pig and wouldn't it be horrible to really see one, and she'd put an anaconda writhing through some high cattail-looking things. All these things were in the rain forests. The rain forests of Brazil . . . what a marvelous sound it had. Her father, who loved music, talked about "tone" sometimes. "It doesn't apply just to music, you know, Polly-o. A *life* without tone is hollow. It lacks resonance." Polly almost knew what he meant, but not quite. She imagined one day she'd know that, and know about other things her parents and grandmother valued and talked about. Perspective. Empathy. Forbearance. She knew what the words meant, because she'd looked them up, but hadn't got around to understanding them yet.

In the southern part of Brazil, there were big herds of cattle. She'd draw two standing cows and one lying down, with a tree spreading its branches—

Rusty and her father came into the kitchen with a quart can of ungraded syrup which was what they used for making maple sugar candy. Her father got out the leaf molds and a big sugar-encrusted pan that Gram had *told* him was to be kept in the shed and not in the kitchen. Polly started to say something, then bent over her map and concentrated on cows.

"Won't be in your way, will we?" her father asked.

"It's all right." She sounded ungracious and couldn't help it.

"We'll try to be quiet."

While they waited for the syrup to boil to the right consistency for pouring, Rusty assailed his father with knock knocks.

"Knock knock."

"Who's there?" said Mr. Lewis, keeping his voice

down as an example to Rusty.

"Cyril."

"Cyril who?"

"Cyril nice to be here. Knock knock."

"Who's there?"

"Harriet."

"Harriet who, keep your voice down, Rusty."

"Harriet a bug and throwed up—"

"Threw up," Polly muttered. "Who wouldn't?"

"Knock knock."

"Rusty, Polly's trying to work, can't you be a—"

"Darn it! You spoiled it. We'll start over. Knock knock."

"Who's there?" Mr. Lewis sighed.

"Hamid."

"Hamid who?"

"Hamid eggs. Knock knock."

"Oh, for Pete's sake!" Polly yelled. She jumped to her feet and stamped out of the kitchen, up the back stairs to her grandmother's room.

"Gram!"

"My word, what is it?"

"Rusty's down there saying knock knock to Daddy until it's like having a woodpecker knocking your brains out and Mom's at her dumb meeting so she can't stop them and you're up here not stopping them, and—"

"Dear me."

"Is that all you have to say? Wouldn't you think Daddy would have more consideration?"

"Your father has his share of that, and more. But you'll have to admit you've been using up the kitchen after supper for your homework for a couple of weeks now.

Probably your father thinks Rusty needs attention, too. Attention of a pleasant kind, I mean. Not the sort he gets from you. Probably George felt that at this particular time Rusty's needs took precedence over yours. You can't stake out the kitchen as your private preserve, Polly."

"I don't."

"You try, dearie. You try."

"The kitchen table is the only place big enough for my map. Can't they see that?"

"The kitchen is the only place where they can make maple sugar. Can't you see that?"

"And they're leaving that boiling pan in the kitchen cupboard, not in the shed the way they're supposed to, did you know that?"

"Polly."

"I suppose you think I'm tattling."

"Think?"

"Oh, Gram. I'm not. I'm just saying."

Polly sat down on the bed where Chino, their cat, was curled in a striped and silvery loop. Just to look at him, just to be here in her grandmother's room, made her feel calmer. She patted the cat, then the old velvet patchwork quilt that had been worked by Gram's mother. Every stitch by hand. It had a lace border brown with age.

"I shouldn't really sit on it, should I?"

"Probably not."

"Then why don't you tell me not to?"

"Don't like to nag. Besides, things are to be used, and my mother would've been the first to agree. I believe she'd quite like the idea of my granddaughter sitting on a quilt she made when I was about your age."

Polly tried to form an image of her grandmother, age nine. Then she tried to picture herself, an old lady of Gram's age. Whatever that was. Not so awfully old. But what remained real was that she was her age and Gram was hers and that was how things were and always would be, even if you knew that was *not* how they were or always would be.

Funny.

"Do you think your mother is in heaven, Gram?"

"If anybody is, I'm sure my mother is."

Polly didn't think that answered her question. "What I want to know is, do you believe in heaven, Gram?"

"I don't know."

"Gram, how can you say that?"

"You asked me something. I answered as truthfully as I can."

"But Gram, you have to believe in heaven. If there isn't any heaven, where's your mother?"

"In me. In you. And your father."

"But don't you believe in God?"

"Yes. I believe in God, and in good and evil. I believe in *life*, but whether I believe it goes on and on forever— I can't answer that. If I believed in heaven, I'd have to believe in hell, wouldn't I? And that I quite refuse to do."

Polly sighed and gazed about the room, at the old, familiar, lovely things. The highboy with serpentine front, the four high posts of the spool bed, the big braided rug, the blue-and-white-striped wallpaper, a little rain-stained under the windows, but pretty. And Gram's wood stove was pretty. An old black cast-iron one with nickel curlicues decorating it. Earlier, Polly had built a

70

small fire in it, so Gram would be cozy when she came upstairs. Polly always built her own fire and Gram's on chilly evenings. She loved coming in at night to a room where a fragrant fire made the stove seem alive. The stove in her own room was nearly new. White cast iron, very modern and nice. She liked her grandmother's best.

Stroking Chino's head, she looked at the pictures on the wall. One in an oval frame of Gram's mother and father on their wedding day, in their fancy wedding clothes. She was sitting down and he was standing beside her and they faced the camera looking very young and stiff and lovely. There were two dark steel engravings that had been, like the wedding picture, in this room as long as Polly could remember. One of the Cathedral of Notre Dame, in Paris, in the rain. One of a village at the edge of the Black Forest, in Germany. Gram's parents had brought them back from their wedding trip.

Polly got up and went to sit at her grandmother's dressing table, looked in the triple glass, adjusting it to study her profile. One by one she picked up the old silver objects on the age-thin linen runner. A hairbrush, long past any use. A hand mirror, so filmed that no matter who looked in it, only a ghost looked out. A buttonhook. Gram's own grandmother had used it to fasten her high-button shoes. Polly toyed with the buttonhook, trying to feel and not only know that her great-great-grandmother had once held its smooth ivory hilt in her hand, as *her* great-great-granddaughter now held it in hers.

Gram kept all these olden things on her dressing table from fondness. Her makeup stuff, and Gram used lots of nice makeup, was in the drawer. Looking at her grandmother, Polly entirely lost the crabby expression that

71

contact with Rusty had put there.

I believe in heaven, she said, but not out loud.

"I've been waiting all day for you to say something about Kate's postcard," said her grandmother. "I know you got one."

"What's there to say? The postcard didn't say anything. I mean, weeks and weeks and now months have gone by and what does she do? Sends a postcard about sea lions and now she's calling herself Katerina."

The postcard had been of some sea lions in the San Diego zoo. Kate had written, "There are lots of these free, I mean loose, in the ocean. We see them all the time and hear them barking. Love, Katerina. P.S. I've decided to be Katerina from now on, so when you write please say Ms. Katerina Willard."

"She says there are loose sea lions in the ocean and I'm supposed to write Ms. Katerina Willard when I write to her, except I'm not going to."

"Now, Polly."

"Well, I'm not. I wrote her a dozen or ten letters when she first left, and all I get is this dumb postcard about sea lions and call her *Katerina*."

"I think Katerina sounds very nice."

"You do?" Polly was surprised into reconsidering Kate's—Katerina's—decision. "I could change my name, couldn't I?"

"She hasn't actually changed it. Her name is Katherine. She's just given it an exotic touch."

"My name's Pauline. How could I give that an exotic touch?"

"Paulette? Paulina?"

"Yuck."

"You could take the name of your favorite character in a book. I remember when I was a girl I tried to get people to call me Elizabeth, because I was so crazy about Elizabeth Bennett, in *Pride and Prejudice*. Nobody did, though. I've always sort of wished they'd respected my feelings about it. But then, people weren't so indulgent of children's feelings when I was a girl. I expect they just thought I was being silly."

"Oh, Gram. I'm sorry."

"Well—it's long past. Now, who's your favorite character in a book at the moment?"

"Ratty," said Polly, and they burst out laughing. Polly had read *The Wind in the Willows* until she knew it almost by heart, and Ratty was her pet person or animal in any book she'd ever read. "I guess I'll stick to Polly. But I'm still not going to write to—to Katerina What's-her-name."

"That's your decision."

"Would you write to somebody who sent you a post-card after you'd sent them a whole lot of letters?"

"Maybe not. It seems a shame. You two were so close."

"Well, like you say, Gram—it's long past."

"*As* I say."

"That's what I meant. Did you know they don't speak Spanish in Brazil? They speak Portuguese. All the *other* countries in Latin America speak Spanish, but not in Brazil." She was pretty proud of her country for being different. "Did you know that?"

"Yes."

"I thought probably you did. Daddy must have some of the maple sugar leaves ready. Let's go down and get some, huh?"

Chapter eight

"You didn't go to Betty Sackett's party the other day, did you?" Faith asked Polly one noontime.

"I didn't know she'd had one."

Polly and Faith and Sandra were having lunch in the little churchyard. Consuela had gone with her mother to Boston (Moya didn't seem to mind taking Consuela away during the school week) so Polly didn't feel they'd be interrupting her. She'd come to think of it as Consuela's graveyard, or her lunchroom, or something, and would have felt funny bringing other people there to eat. And that was funny, too, when you came to think of it.

"Well, Kitty says she had *some* party. She has parties a lot."

"I know," said Polly, who'd never been invited to one. Kate had gone to two, and at one of them there'd been kissing games. Going into a dark closet. Kate had been mucking around in this dark closet, kissing and feeling, and thinking all the time it was Arnie Shawl she had in there with her, and then it had turned out to be Buzz Nickerson.

Yuck.

"Who went?" Polly asked.

"Betty's bunch, and Kitty Trumble and some of her

friends from the Academy, and Cal and Buzz and some other boys. I don't know who all."

"Was Arnie there?"

Sandra looked at Polly over her milk carton. "You got a case on him, Polly?"

"No, I don't have a *case* on him. I like him. He's too nice for Betty and her *parties*."

"Well, Kitty didn't say he was there, so maybe he wasn't. Anyway, the point *is* . . . everybody got drunk."

"You're crazy!" Polly shrieked.

"Well, Kitty said they did. She says she was sick to her stomach when she got home and she was glad her mother wasn't there because then she'd have had to say she'd got sick from something at Betty's party, even if she didn't say what it was that made her sick, and then Mrs. Trumble would've telephoned Mrs. Sackett and it would have got *out*. Everybody would know. Kitty says we can't tell, Polly, so it's a secret, understand?"

"I don't tattle," Polly said coldly. Blabbermouth, yes. Tattletale, no. "You mean nobody found out? Not even Betty's parents?"

"Kitty says that Betty's parents are so used to finding the living room full of kids that they only wave and go upstairs to look at television. Kitty says they never stop, or ask how things are going, or what are you kids doing, or anything like that."

"Drunk," said Polly, unconvinced. "On what?"

"Vanilla!" Faith and Sandra said together.

"Oh, that's dopey."

"Well, it isn't. Kitty says that's what it was, and why should she make it up?"

"How many people were at this party?"

75

"Oh, lots."

"How much vanilla does Mrs. Sackett keep in her kitchen? I mean, does she have it around like maple syrup or something?"

"Everybody had to bring their own, Kitty says. She says Betty told them it was for an experiment."

"How big?"

"How big what?"

"How big a bottle?" Polly said impatiently. "Vanilla comes in a little bottle and a medium-sized bottle and a big bottle."

"Like the three bears," said Sandra.

"I don't know," Faith said regretfully. "We didn't ask. Who would? And now we can't, because Kitty's sorry she told us. She thinks we'll tell someone else and it'll get around."

"Did they drink it right out of the bottle? I should think they *would* be sick."

"No. They made milkshakes and everybody poured their whole bottle in."

"What happened when they got drunk?"

"Kitty says it was awful."

"She says Buzz took his pants down and showed everybody."

"I don't want to talk about it anymore," said Polly.

"And the Sacketts came in, not while Buzz's pants were down, and they just waved and went upstairs. Boy, if my folks came home and found everybody stoned on the cake flavoring, I'd be— They'd be— They'd probably send me to jail."

"Oh, Faith. They would not."

"Maybe to a psychiatrist," said Sandra.

76

"Well, they sure wouldn't trot upstairs to look at *As the World Turns*, let me tell you. And I bet I wouldn't ever give a party again. Or go to one, either," she added. She looked around the churchyard. "It's nice here, Polly."

"It is, really," said Sandra. "You'd think it'd be spooky, but it isn't."

"This is where Connie comes at lunchtime, isn't it?" Faith asked. Polly nodded. "She's a funny girl. I wonder if she'll ever get used to us?"

"My father says her mother's famous," said Sandra. "Betty says that's why she's stuck up."

"Well, she isn't," Polly said. "I mean, her mother *is* famous, but Connie—Consuela's—not stuck up. *Painfully* shy, Gram says."

"Oh well," said Sandra. "Probably someday she'll get over it. Anybody want one of my cookies?"

Polly went home that afternoon in a thoughtful mood. There were things that went on in the world that she didn't know anything about. In fact, things were going on right in her own village that she only found out about by accident. What else was happening, and where? She decided she'd rather not know.

When you thought it over, the worst she had to put up with was Rusty. When you heard about things like that party, Rusty didn't seem such a cross to bear. There were all sorts of crosses she didn't have to bear. She didn't have to be like Consuela, lonely and angry and far from home. She didn't have to go to Betty Sackett's and get sozzled on vanilla and then go home and throw up. She didn't have to kiss *Buzz Nickerson* in a closet.

She was lucky, all right. And maybe the best part was that she knew it. Compared to all that other stuff, Rusty was good news.

When she came into the kitchen she found her brother at the table, working on a jigsaw puzzle. One he'd done before.

"Hi, Rusty," she said cheerfully. "Can I help you with it?"

"I don't need help."

"I mean, can I *do* it with you? We never do things together, and I think we should."

Rusty looked at her doubtfully. "You feeling all right?"

"I feel fine. Wonderful. Why?"

She expected him to say something like maybe she should see a veterinarian, or were the rocks in her head rolling around more than usual, but after a moment he picked up a piece of the puzzle and studied it. "This looks like it should fit here. But it won't."

Polly sat beside him. "It does, doesn't it?" She tried, shook her head. "I always put pieces like that aside and get back to them later. Look, you work the field and I'll take the sky, okay?"

The sky was the hardest part, practically all blue and just a few little clouds to give a clue. Rusty always left it till the end.

"Okay, sure," he said, and they settled down to work together.

That was how their grandmother found them when she came down from her nap.

And Gram, too, didn't say any of the things you might expect people to say. Like "Will wonders never cease." Her eyebrows flew up, but she didn't say anything, just walked around the kitchen, getting out things for dinner, practically on tiptoe, like someone afraid to break a spell.

Chapter nine

On a bright Wednesday afternoon, the Lewises were working out of doors, putting the yard and the gardens in order for winter. Frost had blackened the dahlias, the chrysanthemums had succumbed, and though there were lots of leaves still fluttering on their parent branches, the surface of the ground was covered with them, a patchwork hodgepodge shifting in the breeze.

Polly and her mother were at the side of the house, planting daffodil bulbs on the long grassy slope that fell away to a little stream. The stream itself, a bit farther on, joined the Fiddle River as it flowed under the covered bridge, and the Fiddle went its way. About a mile farther down it cascaded over a bouldery falls into a pool where, in summer, people swam in the chill amber waters. Then it continued on to join the Connecticut River.

Mr. Lewis was raking leaves into an old yellow shower curtain. When he had a curtainful, he folded the corners together and carried his collection into the vegetable garden and dumped it. You had to keep up with leaves at this time of year, and somebody did a little raking every day.

Polly dug a hole, thrust a bulb in, covered it with care.

Hard to believe, now, that she'd ever see this bank of daffodils actually waving in the spring breeze. Winter, which hadn't even arrived yet, lasted so long in Vermont.

She sat back on her heels. The air had an appley, smoky tang, and all the trees were flaming with color, as if some especially brilliant sunset had fallen like a scarf over the hills. Her father said that the glory of the sight was, at base, a sickness. It was the beautiful flush of disease, which was what made the trees near roads so much flashier than those further back in the hills. The trees of Vermont were sick from salt. Salt laid down, winter after winter, so that cars and trucks could maneuver on the icy roads and highways, could keep going without interruption. Salt was slowly killing the trees of all New England, and there didn't seem to be anything that could—or anyway ever would—be done about it.

She looked over at the vegetable garden, where Gram and Rusty were getting in the last of the turnips. In a corner of the garden stood Fafeek, their scarecrow. Pretty soon she and Rusty were going to give him a new head. Most of the year his head was a gunnysack filled with straw and painted with a crazy face. His body had been the same for years. One long stick sticking up and a short stick stuck across. But they changed his clothes from time to time. When he'd weathered a winter, his last fall's outfit was always in tatters, so they'd scrounge around for something new. This year, since spring, he'd been wearing an old bathrobe of Gram's. It had started out red but was now a streaky pink. A pair of scorched and worn-out hot-pad mittens stood stiffly out at the ends of his stick arms, and an old straw sun hat, also Gram's, was crammed down on his burlap head. She and Rusty, shortly before Hallowe'en, always took off the gunnysack head and replaced it with a carved pumpkin face.

Should we have it smiling or scowling this year? Polly wondered. Whichever she decided she wanted, she'd tell Rusty the opposite, and then give in when he argued.

"How's the portrait going?" her mother asked, tamping earth down on the last bulb. "Do you enjoy sitting for it?"

"Well, I don't like the *sitting*. I mean, Moya forgets I'm there, I think. I mean, she's so busy painting me she forgets I'm made of flesh and *bone*. Mostly bone, I think."

Anna Lewis smiled. "Can't you remind her?"

"Oh, well . . . I hate to. She's such—she's so happy when she's painting. She wears a white velvet housecoat—negligee, I mean—and it's all covered with splatters."

"White velvet to paint in?"

"Yes, and she always paints with two brushes, one in her mouth and one in her hand, and she plays music all the time, mostly string music. Did I tell you what Daddy said?"

"About what?"

"I told him how being with Consuela sometimes makes me feel silly and chattery, like a parakeet walking along beside some gorgeous tall bird with a wonderful low voice, and Daddy says I'm a flute trying to sound like an oboe. That was nice."

"Yes, it was. You are rather like a flute, come to think of it. Slender and small and very very sweet."

Polly sighed comfortably.

"But what do you think of the painting?" Mrs. Lewis asked again.

"I haven't seen it yet. She says later on. Let's go help Daddy."

"Whoever invented the leaf rake," said George Lewis as they joined him, "was one mighty clever party. Marvelous, the way it grasps the leaves and glides over the grass."

"If they hadn't invented it," Rusty said, coming out of the garden with Gram, a basket full of turnips between them, "then we wouldn't have to rake leaves."

"Hah. If he hadn't invented it, we'd be obliged to pick up every one of these leaves by hand."

"That's like the stories where the princess has to separate the seeds from the sand," said Polly. "We'd need a flock of birds or a hive of ants to help us out."

"Hive of ants," said Rusty. "Boy, are you ever a dumbbell. Here, lemme help, Dad."

Chino and Okie did their best to undo progress. Chino leaped and rollicked and burrowed, scattering heaps as soon as they were piled. He danced up sideways to Mr. Lewis' rake, scampered away and up a tree, dropped to the ground and began stalking a large maple leaf. Okie tore around barking at the enemy, Rusty's rake. Okie spent his life protecting Rusty from rakes and swings and bicycles and other menaces.

Now, while the rest of them raked, Mr. Lewis spread leaves over the vegetable garden as evenly as possible in the rising breeze. In a couple of weeks, when he had as many leaves there as he wanted, he was going to rototill the soil in preparation for planting peas for early spring.

"Daddy!" Polly shouted. "We can't get anymore! They keep blowing away."

"Okay. Let's quit for the day." He came out of the

garden, closed the gate behind him. "Put the rakes away, kids, will you? I'm going in to tackle those papers."

"And I'm going in to take a nap," said his wife.

"Let's swing, huh, Polly?" said Rusty.

"Okay."

They'd piled a great new mound of leaves under the swing that hung from an old beech tree in the front yard. Every year they put more and more leaves there, yet somehow the mound seemed high for only a little while. Rains would come, and then snow, and by spring the ground there was flat again. But now it was great to swing as high as you could and then let go and sail into the crisp and fragrant hill of oak and beech and birch and maple and sycamore castoffs. Sometimes they got going, then lay back and with a strong thrust somersaulted off the swing into the leaves.

"Give me a push, Poll," Rusty said, seating himself with a wiggle. Okie came rushing up, tongue lolling at the side of his mouth, prepared to take issue with the swing. He seemed to find everything Rusty did a threat of some kind, and his warning bark rang through their days.

When Polly took hold of the sides of the swing, Rusty dug his feet in and said angrily, "I've told you a billion times, *don't* grab the swing! Push me on the *back*. Quit barking, Okie! I haven't even started yet—"

"Daddy always does us by holding the swing."

"He knows how to *do* it. You just topple me off."

"Oh, topple yourself off," Polly said, walking away from him.

"I didn't want to swing with you anyway!" he shouted after her.

"Good. Then we're even."

"What I like," said Gram, coming out of the kitchen with a pail of potato and apple peelings, "is the predictability of you two. No wondering where we all stand. We stand up to our necks in senseless squabbles."

Polly looked at the sky in silence.

"Want to take these up to the pig for me?"

"Sure, Gram."

The pig had been rather a hero a few months before, in the summer, when he'd escaped a roundup for the hog butcher and then had returned some time later, apparently having found that living in the woods by his wits was not a piece of pie. He'd been a young brown boar then, and they'd named him Mocha and Mr. Lewis had been persuaded by Polly and Rusty to winter him over.

What they'd had in mind was that Mocha would turn out to be another Wilbur and live with them forever, a member of the family once removed. But *Charlotte's Web* and Wilbur somehow didn't apply to Mocha, who was now a barrow and getting big, gross, and surly. When he'd been little and living with a lazy sow, there'd been just an electrified wire holding them in their enclosure, but as Mocha grew he seemed to become impervious to electric shock and kept getting out. There'd been three pig chases that nobody had enjoyed, except maybe Mocha and Okie. So now he was behind stock wire, and now everybody except Polly called him just "the pig."

He trundled out of his wallow at her approach and lunged at the trough when she'd dumped the peelings in.

Polly listened to his slurpy gobbling, looked at the round brown sides that were caked with mud, and said in a guilty, self-conscious voice, "Hello, Mocha. How's the nice piggy?"

Piggy crammed and guzzled. When he'd got every last morsel, grunting and snuffling up and down the trough to make sure, he turned and bolted for the wallow as if he couldn't get away from her fast enough.

Polly picked up the pail and walked toward the house, looking at the ground, brooding. Sometimes things were sad. Rusty, who took his turn in feeding Mocha, had entirely lost affection for him, but didn't feel that any blame should be attached to him because of that. He didn't feel disloyal. But after all, Polly thought, *we* were the ones who were crazy about him and wanted to keep him forever, and it isn't Mocha's fault that he's got so unpleasant to be around. It's just the way he's made. Though nothing had been actually said, and despite the promise to winter him over, Polly was sure Mocha would never see the spring. She tried to squeeze out a tear at the thought, but her eyes remained dry, her feelings untouched, and she thought that was what was making her unhappy. Not what was going to happen to Mocha, but realizing she didn't care any more than Rusty did.

"Polly! Come help us decide how to array Fafeek for Hallowe'en!"

There was Moya in the garden with Gram and Rusty and Consuela. They were studying the scarecrow, and Polly joined them without another thought for Mocha.

"Helen says you always change his burlap head for a pumpkin head this time of year," said Moya.

Polly, with only an instant's confusion, realized that there really wasn't anything else that Moya could call Gram, whose name was Helen. She couldn't very well call her Gram, could she—

"What do you say, Polly?"

"About what?"

"Pay heed, poppet. We're wondering if it wouldn't be fun to have a cat's face on the jack-o'-lantern. What do you say to that?"

"I never heard of a cat-o'-lantern. How would we do it?"

"That should be easy enough. We'll make whiskers and pupils in his eyes—"

"How?"

"Make large eyes and leave a piece going down the center. It'll look like Chino's eyes when they're slit against the light. You'll see. Don't you think that'd be fun, Connie?"

"I think it's all fun," Consuela said with unusual animation. "I think it'd be marvelous to dress up a scarecrow. What shall we have him wear?"

"I have an old summer print," said Gram, "that might do." She looked at the streaky pink bathrobe now clothing Fafeek. "He gets good wear from his things, doesn't he?"

"How about my white velvet negligee?" said Moya. "It's served its time for me, and I do think a cat would choose velvet if he were obliged to wear clothes."

"Gee, that'd be beautiful," Polly said. "It's this long trailing gown thing, Gram, that Moya wears to paint in. It's all spattered with beautiful different paint colors."

"You wear white velvet to *paint* in?" Gram asked Moya.

"I wear anything. I do try not to mess up things that are practically new. Oh, my . . . I really can see Fafeek, with his cat's face glowing in the dark. We *can* put a candle in his head, can't we, and dance around him?"

"Don't see why not," said Gram, as if she danced around scarecrows regularly.

"I see his eyes and his whiskery smile shining in the night, and his velvet raiment streaming in the night wind," Moya said happily. "*What* a picture he makes!"

"If there's enough wind to set his raiment streaming," said Gram, "it'll blow out his candle."

Moya looked dashed.

"We could put a flashlight in his head," said Polly.

"Polly! You're brilliant! *What* a superior idea!"

Consuela averted her head, but Gram looked at Moya indulgently. She'd quite come to like her. Moya, said Gram, *had* to dramatize everything. She couldn't help it. Polly wondered if that was why Consuela never dramatized anything. She'd never seen Consuela . . . exuberant.

Consuela and her mother had not only had supper with the Lewises several times, but Moya had taken to dropping in at odd times.

"She's flamboyant, all right," Anna Lewis had said, "but it's nice. She adds a sort of snap and ginger to our lives."

"That makes her a gingersnap!" Rusty had hooted.

Polly knew what her mother meant. There was something sharp and spicelike about Moya O'Shea. And there was, a person had to admit, a kind of flatteringness about how she'd picked the Lewises to like better than anybody else in town. Lots of people were anxious to have her at their house because she was famous. But except for the Lewis family, she didn't seem to want to make friends at all. She stayed up in her house on the hill, painting and reading and listening to music. You'd see her jogging on country lanes in her elegant jump suits, or flashing through town like a big loud hummingbird on her motorcycle. She'd speed off in her Mercedes, Connie beside her, to New York or Boston for the weekend. She was not only like spice—like ginger and cinnamon and cloves— she was also sort of mysterious. Sometimes she talked to children as if they were grown-ups, sometimes talked to grown-ups as if they were children, and she had, said George Lewis, no acquaintance at all with such words as *perhaps* or *somewhat* or *I think*.

"Extremes," said Mr. Lewis. "She deals only in extremes."

"What do you do when you go to Boston or New York?" Polly had asked Consuela.

"Go to art galleries. See people."

Polly had been dying to ask what people, who they were, what they were like, what they did and said and wore and thought about things. But Consuela wasn't somebody you asked questions of. She told you something or she didn't. Polly had sighed, missing Kate— okay, Katerina—acutely and for the first time in ages. Things had been so easy with Kate. They'd talked and talked, the two of them, about everything. Sometimes, of course, about nothing. But it had all been so easy, so much fun.

"The reason we came by," Moya was saying, "is to ask if anybody wants to come along with us while we look at a horse." She patted Fafeek's wooden arm. "We'll get back to you, sir."

"You're going to get a horse?" Polly asked Consuela.

"There's a place has one advertised for sale. We thought we'd go look."

"Who's coming with us? How about you, Helen?"

Gram looked at Moya's Mercedes. "Can't all go in that. If you're willing to go in the truck—"

"Willing? We'd *adore* it. Wouldn't we, Connie?"

Consuela nodded.

"I'm coming too," Rusty said, the first words he'd spoken in ages. Rusty was so smitten with Moya O'Shea that in her presence he became just about mute. He'd fix his eyes on her and practically without blinking keep them there until she was gone from his vision. It would make me nervous as heck, Polly thought, having somebody, even somebody seven years old with a crush, *staring* at me that way. Moya didn't appear to mind in the least, or even to notice most of the time, except now and then to toss Rusty a bright glance of understanding. Polly supposed she'd had lots of male people look at her that way. She was just glad her father didn't.

"Want to ride in back, Moya?" Rusty asked now. "It's swell, riding in back."

"All right, Rusty. I don't hold with turning down a new experience."

"Not me," said Consuela. "It's too cold."

"Cold!" Rusty shouted with laughter. "You think today is cold? Boy, you ain't seen nothin' yet!"

"Pipe down, Rusty." Polly glared at him.

"I'll pipe up all I want to, see!" He scrambled to the back of the truck, voluble in his pleasure at having persuaded Moya to ride with him. He turned and very courteously offered her a hand up.

Gram was smiling as she got behind the wheel and waited while Consuela and Polly got in beside her. "All set?" she said. "They all right back there?"

Polly twisted around to look. "Yup."

"Then where to, Consuela?"

The advertised horse was on a farm a few miles out of town. Gram drove there easily enough because it was also the place where they bought their eggs and chickens in the winter. The Lewises didn't winter chickens, and Polly preferred getting them from Mrs. Barber. She liked gathering eggs, and she liked what her father called the birdbrained behavior of barnyard fowl, liked the sound of their clucking and crowing. But she did not like having them killed.

Mrs. Barber came out of the barn as Gram pulled into the driveway. "Afternoon, Mrs. Lewis. Girls. Want some nice stewing hens today?"

"No, thanks, Mrs. Barber. We've brought some friends to look at the horse you've advertised. This is Ms. O'Shea and her daughter, Consuela."

"How do?" Mrs. Barber inclined her head slightly but gave no indication that she'd heard of the famous Ms. O'Shea. "Thimble's over there in the paddock. If you'll follow me."

Polly blinked when she saw the horse. A smoky-brown, slender mare, maybe twelve or thirteen hands. "That's no old cow pony," she said softly.

"Pure-bred Morgan mare. Hasn't got papers, but she'll go a bit cheaper for that. Eight years old, broke to ride just beautiful. Who's she for?"

"We were just looking—" Moya began, as Consuela, moving to the fence, said, "She's for me."

Moya turned out her hands. "She's for her. As you see. But why are you selling such a lovely animal? Is she— I don't mean to be suspicious, but is she in good condi—"

90

"Never sold anything in my life wasn't in good condition."

"No, no. I didn't mean— I do beg your pardon—"

Polly looked with interest at Moya, who rarely got flustered but certainly was flustered now. Comes of trying to be businesslike, she thought. She probably thinks she should be but doesn't know how to go about it.

"I can understand your question," Gram said. "Your being a stranger here, you need to ask questions. But Mrs. Barber's saying nothing but the truth. Anything you buy from her will be sound."

"Could I ride her a bit?" Consuela asked.

"Wouldn't let you take her, 'less you had. You want me to saddle her up?"

"Oh, no. I mean, thank you, but I'll do that myself."

Mrs. Barber looked at her approvingly. "Tackle's in the barn there, first stall. You bring her over, mind, when you've got her saddled up. Let me check." She opened the paddock gate and Consuela took Thimble's halter and led her out and toward the barn, Polly tagging after.

"What made you change your mind?" she asked, running her hand down Thimble's strong beautiful neck, patting the satin nose, looking into the large brown eyes that regarded her gravely in turn. "She's gorgeous, Connie."

Consuela sighed. She'd apparently been stricken with love at first sight. After a moment she turned to Polly and said, "I just got to thinking it'd be more fun to ride with you than alone."

"Gosh, that's swell," said Polly, a little surprised, but pleased.

When Mrs. Barber had satisfied herself that Consuela knew how to saddle a horse, she nodded and said, "Off you go, then."

"Don't be too long, Connie," her mother called after her. "We have to get back."

Consuela, with her backhanded wave, walked a distance on Thimble, then broke into a light trot.

"Nice seat," said Mrs. Barber. "She'll do."

Moya looked astonished at this, but Polly knew that someone with a horse like Thimble wasn't going to sell her to just anybody who wandered in off the road. There were some things that Moya didn't know about at all.

Chapter ten

Mornings found cattle munching frosty grass. There were skins of ice on puddles, on the water in the pig's trough. The brook flowed free but weeds and grasses at its edge were stiff with rime. Polly, coming out of the house to get her bicycle, watched her breath form on air. She and Rusty were still biking to and from school. Probably they'd continue until sometime in November, when it would begin to get too cold for bicycling. Then someone would drive her the mile and half. There was a school bus she could take, and that Rusty did take, but its route required riding an hour to go ten minutes' worth. Polly didn't use it in the morning. School buses were awful, because of the types like Rusty who rode them. Consuela often used the bus, but for some reason nobody ever teased Consuela, not even dopes like Buzz or Cal. After school, unless it was too bitter even for her, Polly walked home. She bet she didn't ride the bus half a dozen times a year.

Now she stopped a moment to look across the road to the pasture. There, since there was no fence around Moya's property, and no barn, Consuela's mare, Favorita, shared the pasture with Blondel and Mr. Ingalls' herd.

93

("Favorita?" Polly had said. "Why? Thimble's a darling name."

"It's not the name I gave her. I'm naming her for Tía Favorita. She's my aunt and I love her."

"But Thimble's used to being Thimble. You'll mix her all up, calling her something else."

"She won't know the difference." Consuela had looked at Polly and given one of her rare laughs. "Don't look as if I'd insulted you, Polly. I'm not insulting horses, either. They just aren't smart, that's all. That doesn't mean they aren't wonderful."

"Blondel knows his name," Polly said firmly.

"He knows your whistle. And he knows you, of course. They're smart enough to know their people, but I don't think horses even know they've got names."

Polly didn't agree. She didn't argue, either.)

Now she wheeled her bike out of the barn, stood for a moment watching Blondel and Favorita, who were invigorated by the bright air. They raced across the rime-whitened pasture like a couple of foals, teasing the cattle, now and then whinnying as if out of sheer joy. A pair of gorgeous, *intelligent* animals.

Pushing her bike past the garden, she lingered again, to look at Fafeek, splendid in his velvet paint-spattered negligee, with his orange cat's head smiling, and his long black opera gloves sticking out to either side. Polly was sure there had never been another scarecrow to touch him. She opened the garden gate and went carefully between rows where the peas had been planted, climbed the fence on the far side to reach into Fafeek's head and turn off the flashlight they left in there at night. She could see him from her window after she went to bed. The moon was nearly full these nights, so she could see his white robe wraithy and ghostly in the dark and above it his cat's face gleaming.

Moya had come down one evening and taken pictures of him. She'd taken some in the daytime, too. She'd half promised Polly to paint a picture of him that she could hang in her room, but the idea seemed to make Polly's parents uneasy.

"Look, honey," her father had said, "the woman gets thousands for one of her canvases. I don't see how she'd just—make you a present of one." He'd frowned. "I don't figure relationships in terms of bookkeeping, but just the same . . . What do you think?" he'd asked his wife.

"I don't know. I guess artists do dash off sketches for their friends. Polly is certainly Moya's friend. But still . . . I don't know."

Now Polly didn't know either. Until they'd got so hot and bothered, she'd just been pleased at the idea. Well, no point thinking about it. Maybe Moya had just been talking. She often just talked. Once she'd said she'd take Polly to Boston with her and Consuela, but then she'd never mentioned that again. And often she'd said, when Polly had been posing, that she must have "the family" up for supper—she called it dinner—some evening. She never went so far as actually to ask them. Since she'd now had Gram's food several times, probably she was too nervous to cook for them. Gram's cooking affected people that way. At Moya's they didn't actually do what Gram would call cooking. They took things out of the freezer and heated them.

The portrait was almost finished now, according to Moya. Polly had thought it was finished ages ago, but Moya kept dabbing at it here and there. The first time Moya had allowed her to see it, Polly had had to fight to keep from yelling, and Moya had laughed at her.

"Now Polly. You wanted me to make you look *pretty*, didn't you?"

She could scarcely admit that, but just the same—

"Polly, prettiness is paltry stuff. If you were only that I wouldn't be bothered painting you. Loads of girls have pretty faces. Dear little eyes and noses and chins that add up to *nada*. You have character. Presence. What's on that canvas is not a pretty little girl, it's a *person*. Somebody who's going to live a real life—"

Well, that was quite wonderful to hear, and actually each time she looked at the painting, Polly understood it more. In spite of the dark colors and the sort of *smoldering* look, she was beginning to like the girl in the portrait, which was her. A *person*.

Moya had said she didn't need to pose anymore, but Polly had fallen in the habit of riding up there every few days and Moya seemed to like it. Or she did most of the time. A couple of days before, when Polly had ridden up looking for Consuela and Favorita, she'd been a little sharp.

"I don't know where she is, Polly. Where they are. She and the horse. Perhaps Connie felt like being alone for a while. People do need to be alone once in a while, you know. Or do you?"

Before Polly could decide if her feelings were hurt, Moya smiled and said, "Come into the kitchen with me while I practice frying a chicken. I thought I'd start there and work up to coq au vin, and *then* I can have you all for dinner."

Polly arrived at school, put her bike in the rack and went into the yard where some girls were jumping rope.

Cinderella
Dressed in yella
Went downtown to buy an umbrella
On the way she met her fella
How many kisses did she get?
One . . . two . . . three . . . four . . . five . . .

Their voices mingled with those of boys shooting baskets and yelling at one another. Polly had read that here and there girls were joining Little League baseball teams, and that there were some girls even getting on football teams. But in her school the boys and girls separated this way in the school yard and nobody seemed to mind.

She considered whether she had time to join the jump ropers, decided not, and went to her classroom. When the door was closed a little later, Mrs. Hinshaw looked around the room.

"Well, not one absentee," she said. "A record. Mrs. Farquhar will be here for your art period this afternoon. She asked if it'd be all right to take your maps down today, since she plans a Hallowe'en art festival and we'll want to hang your new work on the walls. Suppose we get them down now, before class begins."

Polly's map of Brazil had caused a lot of comment on Parents' Night. It was so big that it took up the space of six other maps, and everybody except Betty Sackett and her bunch said it was marvelous. Betty had trouble thinking anything she hadn't personally done by hand herself was marvelous.

Now, as they moved to take down the maps to make room for the art festival, Arnie Shawl said, "What're you going to do with that, Polly? Hang it in your room or something?"

"I don't know. I mean, I guess I'll just roll it up and stick it away someplace," she said modestly. Actually, she intended to put it up on the wall in the kitchen next to the telephone. She was desperately proud of it.

"I think it's swell," said Arnie. "I was wondering if you'd like to sell it."

"Huh?"

"Well, it's kind of like a work of art, and artists sell their stuff. That's right, isn't it, Connie?"

Consuela nodded. "If they're lucky." Consuela, being modest for her mother, did not say, "If they're good."

"Well, how about it, Polly?" said Arnie. "I mean, if you aren't going to hang it anywhere in your house, I'd like to put it up in my room—"

"Oh boy—listen to that, will you?" said Buzz Nickerson. "*Arnie* wants something of *Polly's* to hang in his *bedroom.*"

There were a few scattered guffaws. Flushing slightly, Arnie said, "Drop dead, Buzz."

" 'Cause *you* say so? In a pig's—ear," he said, glancing at Mrs. Hinshaw. "Let's see you try to make me drop dead, Arnie old boy."

The two of them moved up against each other, scowling. Both were muscular and athletic and they'd tangled before, but Mrs. Hinshaw moved easily between them.

98

"Not on company time," she said, and Arnie laughed. Buzz continued to glare, but stepped back.

"How about it, Polly?" Arnie persisted. "I'll give you a dollar. That sound okay?"

"Sure, Arnie," she said, trying to keep reluctance out of her voice. She'd really wanted to hang it on the kitchen wall. But Arnie was so nice, and she suppposed it was pretty flattering that he liked her map that much.

"Well," said Mrs. Hinshaw. "That was an interesting transaction. Our first art deal. I will say that I think Arnie has a bargain there."

Polly, beginning to be unnerved by attention, took the thumbtacks from the map, rolled it up and handed it to Arnie, who gave her a dollar bill in exchange. Feeling partly proud and partly silly, she thrust it into her sweater pocket, and willed Mrs. Hinshaw to get the class started so everyone would quit looking at her and giggling.

"Shall we get out our arithmetic books?" said Mrs. Hinshaw. Polly sighed, welcoming even fractions, though arithmetic was her least favorite subject.

When Mrs. Farquhar met them in the art room, she offered a choice of paints or clay. "Make some Hallowe'en impression," she suggested. "Anything that comes to mind."

"You watch," Sandra whispered to Polly. "What will come to mind is cats, bats, witches or jack-o'-lanterns."

Polly, who'd taken clay and had planned to model a witch or a cat, said, "How right you are," and burrowed in her mind for some alternative to a cat, a bat, a witch or a jack-o'-lantern. What else was there to Hallowe'en?

Well, there was Fafeek. He had a jack-o'-lantern—that was, a cat-o'-lantern—head. Still, he was a scarecrow, not a witch. She couldn't figure any way to model him, though.

"Could I have paint and paper instead, Mrs. Farquhar?" she asked.

For an hour the class worked on their Hallowe'en impressions. Polly, as she painted Fafeek by night, realized that watching Moya all these weeks had taught her something. Now as she sketched the scarecrow with a bit of the fence behind him and some of the garden in front and then painted Fafeek himself, as ghostly and glimmering as she could manage, with the moon like a wheel in the night sky and his cat's face shining spookily, she felt almost shaky with pleasure. She'd picked up from Moya a feeling for contrasting light parts and dark parts in a painting, a feeling for making one part more important than another—

"Polly. Polly Lewis!"

She looked up to find Mrs. Farquhar smiling at her. "Time's up, Polly. It's a shame to have to stop when you're so caught up in what you're doing." She walked over to look at the painting of Fafeek in the moonlight. "My goodness—that's fascinating, Polly. Really good. I understand you made a sale today, of your marvelous map?"

Polly darted a glance at Arnie and gave Mrs. Farquhar a silly smile. It felt like the *silliest* smile, but she couldn't stop it.

"It's just possible, Arnie, that you've bought the first work of a coming artist."

"Crimers," Betty Sackett muttered. "Coming swell-head is more like it."

Mrs. Farquhar, like all teachers, was good at not hearing what she preferred not to hear. Now she said, "Polly's is far from the only interesting work we've produced today. Shall we take them back to your classroom now and hang the pictures? We'll put the clay models on the windowsills. Tomorrow, when your parents come for the lunchtime costume parade, they'll be able to see what you've done."

Sandra, Polly noticed, had done a clay figure of a cat. Consuela, who hadn't inherited her mother's talent, had done a kind of lumpy clay witch.

The next night, Moya drove Consuela down to the Lewises' so that she could go out trick-or-treating with Rusty and Polly.

Connie wore a gypsy costume contrived from her mother's wardrobe. Neither she nor Moya had been at the lunchtime parade in the school yard. Polly would've bet anything Consuela hadn't mentioned it to her mother, and of course she never had any trouble persuading Moya to let her stay home from school. Now, when the time came, she wouldn't go out to trick-or-treat.

"It's too cold," she said. "I think you're scatty, going out in this cold for some apples and old pieces of candy."

"Boy, you're gonna plain freeze to death this winter," Rusty said. "Someday you'll be found all froze up—"

"Shut up, Rusty," Polly said automatically. Actually, she thought Consuela was sort of a bore about the weather, and that Rusty was right. It hadn't even started to get cold yet, not really cold.

She concentrated on making Scotch-tape claws on her left hand, to go with her cat outfit. The ones she'd worn at lunchtime hadn't lasted the afternoon. With Gram's makeup, she'd drawn cats' whiskers and what certainly looked like cats' eyes on her face. She'd made a tail out of a piece of rope, fluffing the ends. It looked more like a lion's tail than a real cat's, but pretty good just the same. "Gram, cut my claws on my right hand, will you?" she asked. "I can't do them."

Moya, admiring everyone in turn, looked Rusty up and down. "You look great," she told him. He had on one of his father's woolen turtleneck sweaters over his own clothes and it came to his ankles. He wore a ski mask and a pair of hot-pad mittens. "What are you supposed to be?"

"A hand puppet," Rusty squeaked. He bobbed up and down, and bowed. Even Polly admitted that he did look and behave like a puppet. He'd thought the whole thing up himself.

"People here make more fuss over Hallowe'en than we do over Christmas," Consuela said moodily.

"Who's we?" said Rusty. Consuela didn't reply, but *we*, of course, meant Mexicans. Nothing, ever, was going to make an American—a United States American—out of Consuela. Nothing her mother did or said or wanted, nothing that the Lewis family or the beauty of Vermont, or owning Favorita, could offer, would make Consuela anything but a Mexican trapped in the north and longing for home.

"C'mon," Rusty said impatiently. "Let's *go*, Poll."

He and Polly went from the bright warm kitchen to beg in the chilly moonlight of All Hallows' Eve.

Chapter eleven

Polly and Consuela, on Blondel and Favorita, were circling a meadow on a plateau high above Connie's house. They were checking for chuckholes or rock outcroppings, walking the horses carefully. They'd come from the Lewises' pasture, up the hay lane, through the woods, and then up a logging road past the O'Sheas' and so to this broad treeless expanse that a Mr. Mitchell used for growing hay in the summer.

"I thought I'd show you this place once before we have to stop riding," Polly said. "Isn't it marvelous? Look how far you can see."

Sometimes she got the feeling that she could see all of New England from here. You could look across the valley where, in today's windless air, smoke rose straight up, like smoke in children's drawings, from hundreds of chimneys. You could see across the town, with its post office, and their school, and Mrs. Lyle's General Store and the Congregational church, and then across the Connecticut River into New Hampshire. And so to hills beyond hills beyond hills, with ski runs cut into their sides, and roads curving in and out of the trees, highways lying flat out, and bone-bare trees among the evergreens. And always, it seemed, one hawk, circling, circling in the denim-blue sky, shadow skimming beneath him.

"Isn't it marvelous?" she said again.

"Yes. I've already been here."

"Oh," said Polly. "Well, that's nice."

"Probably I shouldn't have told you."

"No, that's all right."

"I was just riding around one day and came out here, that's all."

"It's okay. I just didn't know you had, is all."

They continued walking, circling toward the center of the meadow.

On the way up they'd passed Moya in a sky-blue jogging suit, coming toward them. Polly had started to rein in, but Consuela kept going and Moya just smiled and flipped her hand as she trotted past.

"Your mother," Polly said now in a deliberate voice, "is awfully beautiful."

"You said you wanted to show me this place once before we have to stop riding. Why do we have to stop?"

"I told you," Polly snapped. "Hunters. The season on deer begins next week and some of them jump the gun. Riding in the woods when those people are out is like asking to be shot dead. Or have your horse shot, anyway."

"How long does hunting last?"

"Sixteen days. I give it a month, a week on each side, to be safe. Not that you're ever really safe from them. One time a man got shot in the arm while he was in his living room looking at television."

"How do we exercise the horses?"

"We can ride them into town. And they can race

around the pasture together. When it's cool like this, they do a lot of running on their own."

"Are they safe in your father's pasture?"

"Oh, yes. Hunters go into the woods."

"Then how did the man get shot in the arm looking at television?"

"For Pete's sake, Connie. I guess some person didn't go into the woods far enough. I don't know how he did, he just did. And the horses are as safe in the pasture as anyone is during hunting season, that's all I know."

"You're cross because I didn't say my mother is beautiful. Okay, she's beautiful."

Polly took a breath and plunged. "You don't like her, do you?"

She'd been wanting to ask this for a long time. She was being rude. It was none of her business. But if you saw people as much as they saw Consuela and Moya, didn't that sort of give you a right to ask rude questions that were none of your business? Probably not. She waited, half expecting Consuela to ride off and leave her.

Tremendous pause. Finally Consuela said, "She took me away from Mexico. And my father."

"You were living in Texas."

"Texas isn't all that far from Guadalajara, *and* from everybody in the world that I care about."

I asked for it, Polly thought. She leaned over and patted Blondel's neck. "I don't think there're any chuckholes. Let's gallop."

She touched Blondel's flank with her heel and took off across the meadow. The cold air poured sparkling into her lungs, her hair flopped against her neck, Blondel's mane flipped sideways and the sound of his hooves hitting the hard earth was to her hearing like the music of Mozart to Gram and her parents. It was one of the most glorious sounds she would ever know, and she knew it.

She heard the fast hollow thud of Favorita following, and thought she heard, through the wind whistling past her ears, Consuela's voice. "Polly! Polly, stop!"

Favorita, younger and faster than Blondel, pulled up beside them.

"Polly, stop! I want to tell you something!"

Polly brought her horse down to a canter, to a trot, to an ambling walk. "You don't have to say anything. It's how you feel. You can't help how you feel."

"That's not how I feel. Not the way it sounded. It came out wrong. I was thinking about home—I mean, about the ranch, and about Tía Favorita, and I just said something and it came out wrong. Don't you ever do that?"

"Sure."

"Well then. Anyway, I like your grandmother and your parents a lot. An awful lot. And I like you," she said, to Polly's surprise. She was pretty sure, in fact, that Connie did sort of like her, but wouldn't have expected her to say so.

"You're the only friend I have up here," Consuela said. "I mean, that's not the only reason I *like* you—I just mean . . . Oh, I don't know what I mean. Except I didn't mean to hurt you."

"I'm not hurt."

But she had been. She wondered about Moya, who always seemed so cheerful and good-humored. Didn't Moya, even if she didn't show it, get hurt by this girl who could say a thing like that, not meaning it?

106

"Do you want to gallop some more?" Consuela asked.

"I don't know. Do you?"

"I guess not."

They turned their horses' heads toward home.

Chapter twelve

It had become a practice that Moya and Consuela should come for supper at the Lewises' on Friday evening. On the Friday before Thanksgiving they arrived early, bringing into the kitchen a shining aura of outdoor cold. Moya's cheeks, when she leaned over to kiss Polly (she always kissed everybody when she arrived and when she left) were cool, mingled with the delicious fragrance she always wore. She had on a brown wool suit, a creamy sweater with a cocoa-colored scarf at her throat, high tan suede boots, and a hat that looked like beaver but wasn't. Moya wore only imitation furs. Consuela was dressed for twenty below, though it was only twenty above. Rusty was right, Polly thought, you couldn't help wondering what Connie was going to do when it actually got cold.

"I've brought you all a present," Moya said, handing Gram a flat parcel wrapped in brown paper, about two feet by three.

Gram and Anna and George Lewis looked at the parcel warily, and then at Moya, who regarded them happily. I'll bet she's brought us a painting, Polly decided. For the past couple of weeks, Moya hadn't let her see what was on the easel. It was this, Polly said to herself.

She was painting this for a surprise.

Gram put the package on the kitchen table, slowly undid the string, carefully laid back the paper.

"It is!" Polly shouted. "I guessed it was!"

"Oh, boy," said Rusty. "*Lookit*. That's neat, Moya. That's super neat." He was still crazy about Moya, but sufficiently used to her now so that he didn't go dumb in her presence. "That's us, isn't it?"

It was a painting of Fafeek in the moonlight. Moya had put him to one side, in the background. In the foreground were a cat and a gypsy dancing, and a hand puppet leaning over the fence.

"It's lovely," said Gram. "It is simply, absolutely lovely. Mysterious and gay, and— Oh, my, just beautiful."

"Well, it is," said George Lewis. "Marvelous—"

"Acrylics, of course," said Moya. "No oils, or it wouldn't be dry." She looked at the painting with obvious delight.

"But see here, Moya," said Mr. Lewis. "How can we accept this? I mean to say, it's like having Georgia O'Keeffe wander into your kitchen and say, 'Here's something I dashed off for you.' "

Anna Lewis started to say, "*I* think—" as Moya said, "In fact, Georgia O'Keeffe does exactly that. With friends. I know a doctor in New York that she's given two or three to. So there. I interrupted you, Anna."

"I was just going to say that *I* couldn't possibly refuse it. I'd *fight* for it."

"*There*," said Moya to Polly's father. "Besides, you can call it a bread-and-butter painting, if you wish. The only time Connie and I get to eat the way we eat here is when we eat here. On Fridays my body buzzes with delight all day, knowing how sumptuously it's going to be treated come evening. What's for tonight, Helen?"

"Boiled beef with horseradish sauce, spinach salad, pepper jelly, whole wheat rolls, chess pie."

"Oh, I faint. I *swoon*. . . . Rusty, catch me before I hit the floor!"

"Okay, Moya," Rusty said with a grin. "I'm set." He held out his arms.

"On second thought, eat first, swoon later."

"You're trying to divert us," said Mr. Lewis, "from the fact that you've given us a—" He stopped, looked at his wife, his mother, Moya O'Shea. He looked at his children. "Well, it's a magnificent present, Moya. We thank you."

"Good. I'll take it back with me tonight, however. Connie and I are going to New York over Thanksgiving. I want to take the portrait of Polly to my dealer, and I'll have him frame this at the same time."

"We could have it framed," Anna Lewis said.

"Oh, no, no, no, no. A present of a picture comes framed."

"You're going to take Polly's picture to your dealer?" Gram asked.

"My, yes. I think it's one of the best things I've done recently. He must see it." She laughed. "You should *see* your expressions! You all look so *polite*."

Mr. and Mrs. Lewis and Gram had gone up one afternoon to Moya's to see the portrait of Polly. Although Polly, maybe from weeks of association with it, or maybe just because it was a picture of herself, had come to be fascinated by it, her grandmother and parents had looked at it, and then assumed the courteous expressions they wore now.

"Very interesting," George Lewis had said. "Very very interesting."

Since her father didn't hold with the use of the word *very* even once in a sentence, Polly could tell he was at a loss for words. Gram had just stood, nodding her head in an encouraging way, as if Moya's spirits would need to be kept up, and Anna Lewis had said helplessly, "There's definitely something of Polly in there."

Moya had laughed, as she laughed now. When I grow up, Polly thought, I'm going to be like her. I'm going to be that *sure* of myself. She'd decided, besides, that she was probably going to be an artist. Ever since Hallowe'en, when she too had painted Fafeek in the moonlight, she'd felt that was what she'd like to be. Well, maybe she'd decided earlier, during those times when she'd sat for Moya. Or maybe as far back as the days when she'd adored coloring books. The atmosphere of being an artist seemed to her the most wonderful thing she could imagine. The music playing. Moya, in her outfits of tacky glamor, humming with the brush between her teeth, looking so absorbed, so fierce. So happy.

Besides, it was fun to paint. After Hallowe'en, Polly had bought, with her own money, a drawing pad and some charcoal and paints. Afternoons, after school, she'd been experimenting, trying to do a portrait of Gram.

"Old Polly's trying to be an artist, too," Rusty said now. "She stinks. Gram oughta sue her for what she's doing, making her look like an old dead cow."

"Rusty!" said Gram. "Now, Polly, keep your temper—"

111

"Goodness," said Moya. "Polly isn't going to lose her temper because somebody says her work stinks. There wouldn't be *any* artists if that was all it took to stop them."

Polly kept her temper.

"May I see what you're doing?" Moya asked her. "I'd really like to."

"Later," said Polly. "After this toadstool has gone to bed."

"Yeah, I'll go to bed when I want to, you horse's rear end. I'm gonna put a hecks on you, that's what I'm gonna do."

"You halfwit, you don't even know what a hex is."

"I do too so know. It's a curse, Dad said. A spell you lay on somebody you wanna curse."

"You can't lay a spell on somebody if you can't spell what you're laying on them."

"How do you know how I'm spelling my spell, huh?"

"Spell it, then. Spell hex."

"H-e-c-k-s. There."

"It's spelled h-e-x, and you couldn't put a spell on a barn door."

"You know," said Moya, "if I lived with you two, I'd move out. Brawl and bicker, that's all you do. You'd bore the bonnet off me."

Polly and Rusty stared at her, and everyone else began to laugh, even Consuela.

For a girl who'd just decided to be completely sure of herself, Polly was having a hard time. As for Rusty, he scowled at Moya before stamping out of the room. "And I'm not coming back either, see! I'm gonna stay in my room *all night*."

"Oh, dear," said Moya. "I'm sorry." She didn't look in the least sorry. She looked amused. "Will he really stay up there all evening?"

"He'll be down in no time," said Gram. "Let's get dinner on, shall we?"

Fridays they ate in the dining room now, with a fire in the big Defiant wood stove and flowers on the table. Usually there were flowers on the kitchen table, too, but dining-room eating was different, and Polly liked it.

As they took their places, Rusty came crashing down the back stairs, pounded across the kitchen into the dining room, hurled himself into his seat. "Did you say chess pie, Gram?"

Rusty, thought Polly as her mother said grace, really *doesn't* sulk or get his feelings hurt. Just blows up like a firecracker and then comes together again as if nothing had happened at all. Instead of *planning* to be sure of himself, it appeared that Rusty already was. She wondered glumly if it was possible to *become* that way, or did you have to be born like that?

Moya sampled the sauce, closed her eyes and sighed. "This is *Lucullan*."

"No, it isn't," said Rusty. "It's boiled beef."

"Lucius Licinius Lucullus," said Mr. Lewis, "was a Roman consul who apparently set the best table in the history of the empire. Thus, any delicious food can rightly be termed Lucullan."

"Helen," Moya went on, "as a chef you are the topmost berry on the tree. I doubt Lucullus knew better. These rolls! That sauce! Those tender teeny carrots!

113

Never would I have thought I'd relish a carrot. And oh, the green of the pepper jelly! The way it bites the tongue tip!"

"You gonna swoon now, Moya?" Rusty asked.

"After the chess pie, Rusty."

"Well, Consuela," said Mr. Lewis, "what will you do in New York over Thanksgiving?"

He believed in addressing Consuela directly two or three times an evening. "If somebody doesn't," he'd pointed out one Friday after Moya and Consuela had left, "the girl would never speak at all. Does she talk in school yet, Polly?"

"Not very much. And Mrs. Hinshaw doesn't call on her. Betty and that bunch can't stand her. They say she's stuck up because her mother is famous. That's the sort of dopey thing they would think."

"If you didn't know Consuela, do you suppose you might think the same?"

Polly had thought a moment, then nodded. "I guess maybe."

"Consuela isn't easy to know, and I gather you're the only one who's made an effort, which is why you've become friends."

Polly wasn't sure she and Consuela had become friends. Consuela wasn't a person you told things to that you wouldn't tell to anyone else, the way she and Kate had told each other things. If Consuela went away, it wouldn't be the way it had been when Kate had left. Polly had plenty of friends at school now, always someone to eat with, play games with, gab on the telephone with. She didn't need Consuela, the way she'd needed Kate. Just the same, she thought that very slowly they were working their way toward a friendship. She found it all too complicated to discuss, though, even with Gram. So she was just letting matters take their course.

Her father was waiting for Consuela to respond to his question about New York, looking at her in what Polly always thought of as his "teacherly look." A kindly, *encouraging* look.

"We go to museums and art galleries," Consuela said. "And see Mother's friends."

Moya's eyes widened. "That certainly sounds grim, the way you put it."

"It's what we do. I didn't mean I don't like it." But everyone could tell that was what she'd meant.

"Oh, dear," said Moya. "Oh, dear, oh dear. Here I've been thinking you enjoyed our jaunts."

"I do, in a way. I *said*. I like the drive, and cities are nice, like Boston and New York, especially Boston. But it's just—" She fell silent.

"I do not seem to be able to do the right thing, do I?" Moya looked distressed. "I did think I was getting better about galleries and so on. I don't stay nearly as long as I used to, now do I, Connie? Connie's idea of going to a museum," she said to the others, "is three paintings, two statues, and let's have lunch."

"Mother's idea," Consuela said unexpectedly, "is let's stand in front of this Matisse till dinnertime, and then we can come back in the morning and move on to the Cézanne."

"Oh, *honey*," said Moya.

"Well, I get tired."

"I have an idea," said Anna Lewis. "Why doesn't Connie spend the Thankgiving holiday with us?"

115

Chapter thirteen

It was the day before Thanksgiving, and Moya, having dropped Consuela off at the Lewises', had left for New York City.

Polly and Consuela went up to Polly's bedroom.

"Which bed is yours?" Consuela asked, putting her big many-colored Mexican raffia carryall on the floor.

"This one," said Polly, sitting down. "That's Kate's." She frowned. "That's not what I meant, the way it sounded. I mean, we always used to call it Kate's bed. She's the only one who's ever slept in it. Except you, now."

"Why? Is it sacred or something?"

"Of course not. She was my best friend, that's all. I told you."

"You have other friends."

"Yes. I do. Only not like Kate. Gram says Kate and I shut other people out. We grew up together and we did everything together, and then when she left—" She lifted her shoulders, then smoothed Chino's round silky head. He'd followed them upstairs, attracted by the raffia bag. Now he lay on Polly's bed, purring and idle. Polly was pleased to have him here. Except for nights, when he slept with Gram, Chino usually spent the winter either outdoors, where the bitter cold didn't appear to trouble him, or under the woodstove in the kitchen, where the scorching heat didn't seem to trouble him either.

She watched Consuela putting her things away in the bottom bureau drawer that Polly had emptied for the purpose. An Irish wool sweater. A long flowery challis nightgown. Cream-colored snuggies. Three cashmere turtlenecks, a yellow, an ivory, a brown. Such pretty clothes they wore.

"You miss her a lot, don't you?" Consuela said.

"Not as much as I used to. She's Katerina now. Only I keep forgetting. You can hang your skirts and slacks in the closet. I cleared a place for you."

"Thank you. That was nice of you."

Polly let out a long silent inside sigh. This was Wednesday afternoon, and it was a long time till Sunday evening, when Moya would be back. If she and Consuela were going to be this stiff and careful from now till then, it looked like it was going to be a very long holiday.

Consuela finished unpacking, looked around the room, eyed the bed tentatively and then sat on the windowsill.

"Connie!" Polly said. "I'm sorry I made you feel that way, and it is *not* a sacred bed. Please, sit on it like you belonged there. After all, you're going to have to sleep in it. Either that or on the floor, aren't you? We'll call it Consuela's bed, okay?"

Consuela smiled. "That would be nice." She looked around the room. The walls, covered with flowery wallpaper, sloped to two dormer windows that overlooked the meadow at the back of the house and the vegetable garden to one side. The chest of drawers was painted

117

white, the beds had brass head- and footboards and were covered with patchwork quilts.

"Those are pretty," Consuela said.

"Gram's mother made them. We have about six. Wait'll you see Gram's, the one on her bed. It's beautiful."

There was an old braided rug nearly covering the floor and a small cretonne-covered chair. Consuela looked slowly, studying each part of the room. The white cast-iron stove. Polly's picture of Fafeek, framed and hanging near the door. A small marble sink in one corner. The ceiling angled down over it.

"Can you use that?" she asked Polly.

"I used to be able to. I'm getting too tall," Polly added happily.

Consuela, inches taller than Polly, said, "I'd have to get down on my knees." She looked pleased when Polly giggled a little. "This is such a nice room. Such a really pretty room."

"Not nicer than yours." When it's tidied up, she thought. Which it hardly ever was.

"Mine's always a mess. Maybe I'll start keeping it neat. This room is so old-fashioned. It looks like pictures in a book. Like a little room in a Beatrix Potter book."

"I *love* Beatrix Potter." Polly glanced at her bookshelves under the window seat. "I'm saving mine for when I get married and have children. If I get married and have children."

"Don't you think you will?"

"I don't know. Maybe I'll stay here with Gram and Mom and Daddy."

"But—"

118

"But what?"

"But you sound as if you think everything will always stay the same. Things don't always—"

"Don't say it," Polly said shrilly.

"Oh . . . I'm sorry. Really."

"Besides, suppose I had a kid like Rusty?"

"Why don't you like him?"

"He's a pain in the neck and he always has been and I don't see signs that he's going to stop being one."

Consuela thought a moment. " I think he's pretty nice," she said.

"Wait till you've been around him for five days," said Polly, but realized that if Consuela had agreed with her she wouldn't have liked it one bit. Crazy. "I think being a human being is plain crazy."

"I think so too. Except once you get started there's nothing to do about it. I think being a horse would've been more fun. I mean, a horse somebody *cared* about."

"Or a bird. Then you wouldn't care if anyone cared about you. Do you suppose a horse or a bird knows that it is one?"

"I used to wonder about that sometimes, when I looked in El Cometo's eyes. 'Do you know you're a horse and I'm a girl?' I'd ask him. But how could anybody figure out if they know what they're being while they're being it? Do Favorita and Blondel and El Cometo *know* that they're horses, or do they just go along being horses without thinking about it?"

"It'd be nice to know. But I guess we never will. Unless someday we learn to talk to porpoises, then maybe they could tell us." She rubbed Chino's chin, stroking the delicate jawbone beneath the soft fur. "Look at him.

Just lying there getting his chin rubbed, and that's all there is to it for him." And Mocha, she thought, went to slaughter last week with no idea of what was in store for him. She hadn't much liked him toward the end, but was glad he had never had to know what was going to hit him.

But oh—what Consuela had just said was true. Her parents, *Gram*, would not always be here for her to live with, *be* with. This house, the way they were, it wouldn't last all her life. Sometimes she had nightmares about that. But it was far, far away, the change that had to come. She didn't have to think about it for a long, a very long time. And if she had a nightmare, she could always go climb in bed beside Gram. *Always* . . . what a scary word.

"Consuela, let's go downstairs," she said, jumping up. "Let's go find somebody down there and do something with them."

In the kitchen they found Polly's father making bread, something he did almost as well as his mother did. He was kneading dough in a satiny mound, slapping and pounding it with gusto. Gram was making stuffing for the turkey. From the living room came the sound of Copland's *El Salon Mexico*. "Put that on for you, Consuela," said Mr. Lewis.

The kitchen smelled of sage and apples and yeast and wood burning. It was warm and safe and altogether marvelous here in this kitchen, Polly thought, with these people, that music, those odors. When Chino walked in, tail in the air, yelling for food, she laughed out loud.

"Where's Mom?"

120

"She and Rusty have gone over to Mrs. Barber's for the turkey."

"Oh. Should I make the cranberry relish now, Gram?"

"That's a good idea. Consuela can help you."

"Okay. C'mon, Connie. First we have to go down in the cellar and get some apples. Then I'll show you how to make my superior cranberry relish."

In the late afternoon, Consuela and Polly walked across the road with pails of mash for the horses. Polly blew on her whistle and they came, Blondel in the lead. Favorita could outrun him, but seemed to have accepted him as leader. Sometimes Polly wondered why. Because she thought he was wiser as well as older? Or because he was a male?

The two girls sat on the fence, looking at the horses. Consuela was humming some bars from *El Salon Mexico*. She's more like her mother than she'd ever admit, Polly thought. They have ways that are the same. A habit of humming. A way of looking sideways at a person that Mr. Lewis said was entirely fetching. Gestures. Moya had that same backward flick of the hand when she was leaving somebody.

The sun, bright until a couple of hours ago, had disappeared. Gradually the sky was turning gray as tin. It seemed to get heavy, closer to the earth, as dark skies did. It was cold. Since for once Consuela was not complaining, Polly sat on. She thought it was probably going to snow.

Across the road, Rusty and Okie were racing around the lawn, falling over each other, making a lot of joyful

121

noise. Polly turned around on the fence and faced her house, her home, her *place*. She was sure this was how Consuela felt about that ranch in Guadalajara. It must be very hard for her.

But Consuela, at the moment, seemed to be thinking only about where she was, not where she usually longed to be.

"Look at Fafeek," she said. "Do you suppose he likes having his burlap head back?"

Fafeek's cat-o'-lantern head had shriveled to an evil smile and had been fed to Mocha, now gone himself. The white velvet negligee was looking shabby. He was wearing one of Rusty's old ski caps, which went oddly with his opera gloves. "Positively, he looks like a scarecrow," said Polly, and enjoyed Consuela's laugh.

All at once, though in fact the warning signs had been coming for some time, a haze of snow, almost an illusion of snow, filled the air. In moments it thickened and the house across the road was obscured as though behind a thin veil, not yet white, not any color yet.

Consuela gripped Polly's arm. "Polly! What's *that*? Is that *snow*? Is it snowing? Is it really going to snow?" Her voice was hoarse with excitement.

"Yup." Polly lifted her face to the cold vaporous flakes. "Probably hard."

"Oh, Polly! You're marvelous!"

"Well, I didn't actually *do* it," Polly said modestly, proud of Vermont for producing something that could animate Consuela. "Haven't you ever seen snow before?"

"Never. Never in all my life. I've seen it in pictures, and at the movies. But real live *snow*! I can't be*lieve* it, Polly. Do you really think there will be a lot, a *real* lot?"

122

"It seems like the sort of day, like the sort of begin-ning, that turns into a lot," Polly said cautiously. She didn't want to dash Consuela's hopes, but on the other hand didn't want to get them too high. The first time Vermont had done anything to please her, it had raised Consuela to such a pitch that Polly began to be afraid it couldn't follow through.

"Let's go tell everybody," said Connie, leaping down from the fence. "Maybe they haven't seen it yet."

Amazed, Polly picked up the pails and followed as Consuela raced toward the house.

"It's *snowing!*" she shouted, bursting through the kitchen door, a messenger with news of triumph. "Every-body come look! There's snow!"

Gram and Mr. and Mrs. Lewis left what they were do-ing and crowded out on the porch to see the snow as if they, too, were encountering this wonder for the first time.

As they watched, the flakes whitened, thickened, be-gan to fall more rapidly. They swirled to one side, to the other, sometimes drove straight up again and then re-sumed their downward drift. A car, coming carefully down the hill, left dark tire marks behind it in the thin white covering on the road.

"It won't stop, will it?" Consuela breathed. "It's going to go on snowing?"

George Lewis laughed. "Consuela, once it's begun to snow in our part of the world it doesn't stop until May."

"Isn't that wonderful," Consuela said softly, and though Polly knew that Gram and her parents did not entirely agree, they said nothing.

By evening, their part of the world lay muffled in

white, and still the driving flakes fell in their intricate and individual billions. During supper they listened to the wind moan around corners like a bassoon. Afterward, Polly and Consuela put on jackets and went out on the back porch, powdered white almost to the door. Drifts sloped toward the back steps, piled against the sides of the barn. Trees near the house were sweatered in snow and those farther off were tall muffled ghosts. There'd been almost no traffic for hours, but now at the top of the hill a halo of light appeared, spread, then concentrated into a broad ray pointing skyward. It angled, dipped, became the headlights of a truck inching its way downhill toward the covered bridge. Snowflakes mixed and twisted in the two long beams. The truck went past, tire chains clanking. They heard the slap and rumble of chains on the wooden planks of the bridge, then the sound of the truck laboring up the grade at the other side.

"Made it," Polly said. "Good thing he has chains."

Silence again, except for the sifting flakes, the sighing wind.

"How can you hear something so *soft*?" Consuela whispered.

"Will the horses be all right?" she asked, when they'd gone back into the kitchen and were holding their reddened hands over the stove.

"Oh, sure. They like it. If it gets too deep they can go across the pasture to where the trees are. There're always sheltering places in the trees."

Mr. Lewis had built a fire in the living room, and for a while they all sat in there together. Rusty and his father were playing checkers. Gram leaned back in her chair, looking supremely and happily idle. Mrs. Lewis was at the piano, touching the keys softly. There were nice words to the lovely air she was playing: . . . "O'er the quiet meadow, who comes at close of day . . . silent and slow . . . all dressed in mantle gray. . . ?" Mantle gray. That sounded nice. Polly wondered if there could be mantle white. She didn't see why not.

"If you could be an animal," she said suddenly, "what would you be?"

"If who could?" her grandmother asked.

"Anybody. All of us. What would everybody be?"

"I wouldn't be an animal at all," said Gram. "I'll agree a human being isn't always the best or wisest of creatures, but a human being is what I choose to be."

"Gram, you aren't playing it right. It's only an *if. If* you had to be one, then what?"

"I'd be a dog," said Rusty. Polly opened her mouth, closed it. "And you were going to say I'd be a pig, weren't you? Well, I wouldn't."

"I guess you wouldn't," she admitted. "You're too good-looking to be a pig." Rusty stared at her. "You'd make a good rooster. Strutting and crowing."

"I *said* I was gonna be a dog."

"Okay. Be one."

"How about you, Mom?" Rusty asked. "What would you be?"

Mrs. Lewis turned from the piano. "Well, let's see . . . a mountain goat, I think. I'd live way up on some craggy height and spring from rock to rock and nibble edelweiss. That'd be wild and free."

"I've changed my mind," said Gram. "I shall be a tree sloth. I'll hang by my feet and snooze my hours away."

"You'd be bored senseless in half an hour," said her son.

"Not when I'm a sloth. It'll suit me fine."

"How about you, Daddy?" Polly asked.

"Could I read?"

"Read? You're an *animal*. How can you read?"

"I can't give up reading, so I shall have to be an animal that reads. I shall be Ratty. Sit beside the fire in my velvet smoking jacket, reading and writing poetry. How about you two girls? What's your choice?"

"Consuela would have to be—"

"Why not let her tell us, honey?"

"I was going to be a horse," Consuela said happily. "But I've changed my mind. I'm going to be a house cat. In this house."

"Now, there's a compliment for you," said Mr. Lewis. "You'd be welcome to purr on our hearth anytime."

"You certainly would be," said Gram. "And you, Polly-o? You started this. What form do you opt for?"

"I think a bird. A hawk, or an eagle. A bird that could fly way high up for hours and hours and hours."

"Yeah," said Rusty. "That'd be neat. Maybe I'll be that instead of a dog. If it's okay with you, Poll," he added anxiously.

George Lewis put back his head and laughed, and they were all laughing.

Later, when they went upstairs, Polly let Consuela have the first bath. While she waited, she turned down the quilts, fluffed the pillows, put an extra blanket at the foot of each bed. She put one last log in the stove, to keep the room from getting too cold during the night.

126

The lamp between the beds shone softly, and Polly looked around with satisfaction. Gram had taught her to make a room welcoming this way. Gram had taught her so many things. With some deliberation, she selected *The Tailor of Gloucester* to put on Consuela's side of the night table. Connie would have brought her own books, probably. But Gram said you always selected one right book for your guest. *The Tailor of Gloucester*, on such a night, seemed the right book.

When Consuela came in from the bathroom, a yellow woolly sashed robe over her flowered nighty, she paused with the brush halfway down her long black hair.

"It's so *cozy*, Polly. It's like being back on the ranch. There's no beautiful snow down there, but when you go into your bedroom at night it's like this, with the bed turned down and everything looking so—cozy," she said again.

With Moya and Connie's sort of housekeeping, Polly was sure the beds didn't get turned down at night. She wondered if they got made in the morning.

"Who does it for you down there? In Guadalajara. Your aunt?"

"No. The maids."

"I see. Well, why shouldn't you do it yourself up here? I mean, you *could* make it nice in your room and your mother's room at night. I do for Gram. I light her fire and turn her bed down and put her lamp on, so when she comes upstairs she feels *welcomed*."

Consuela slowly resumed brushing her hair. "I could, I suppose. I never thought of it."

"I guess I'll take my bath. See you in a bit."

When she came back, Consuela was on the window

seat, *The Tailor of Gloucester* on her lap.

"You still afraid of the bed?" Polly asked.

"Oh, no. I just like it here, looking out. This is such a nice book. I love the pictures in it. I love being here, Polly."

"That's nice."

"There's so much fun, with your family. Look, Polly, there's a light down there. See how the snow looks, going past that light."

Polly glanced down at the yard, where her father had left the light on over the henhouse. He never left lights on by mistake, and Polly knew he'd done it just so Connie would see the snowflakes falling past that globe of light. They fell thickly and, in spite of the wind, almost straight down until they came out of the surrounding darkness into the circle of lamplight, when they began to toss and sparkle, to go sideways and upward, as if those few millions of flakes were caught in a bright cage. Beneath the light, they seemed released and drifted down in the dark.

Leaving Consuela on the window seat, Polly got into bed. She put her arms behind her head and stretched. "Are you going to come back from Guadalajara?" she asked.

"What?"

"Are you going—"

"I heard. What do you mean, am I going to come back? Of course I'm going to come back. What makes you think I wouldn't come back?"

Polly waved her hands. "I don't know. The way you talk about it, about Mexico, all the time. How you feel about it. I just got to wondering one day if maybe when

128

you got down there at Christmas you just plain wouldn't come back up here."

"That's—that's silly, Polly. Anyway, Papa and Tía Favorita wouldn't let me."

"Oh."

"It isn't part of the arrangement. The arrangement is I live with my mother and go to Mexico for vacations. Papa is not the sort of man who'd let me go against the arrangement that had been made."

Having gone this far, Polly decided she might as well go a bit further. "Would you stay there if you could? If they'd let you?"

Consuela gazed out the window for a long time. Polly was about to give up and start reading, when she turned and said, "No, I wouldn't."

Polly waited.

"I wouldn't because—I think it's right to keep the arrangement, too, when it's been made. Anyway . . . I think she'd be lonely. After all, she *is* my mother. Besides," she went on when Polly said nothing, "I'd miss it *here*. All of you."

"I'm glad." Polly thought of pointing out something she'd noticed that maybe Consuela hadn't, which was that they'd been talking away to each other all evening. With more silences than had ever fallen between her and Kate, but easy silences, and that was okay, too. But she didn't say it. Once in a while she knew when she'd said enough.

Consuela got into bed and for a while they read their books. Finally Polly yawned. Her book slid to the floor. Out in the dark a snowplow was growling down the road like a rhinoceros.

"What's that *noise?*" Consuela asked.

"Snowplow," Polly muttered into her pillow. She yawned again. "So we can—get out in the—in the morning. . . ." In another moment she was asleep.

But Consuela stayed awake for a long time, listening to the snowplow, and the wind, and the snow as it swept against the windows.